Welcome to Shepherds Pass

Alex Mitchell

Published by Alex Mitchell, 2023.

WELCOME TO SHEPHERDS PASS

First edition. October 1, 2023.

ISBN: 979-8891980006

Written by Alex Mitchell.

Chapter One

The average speed of a .22 caliber long rifle bullet is 1082 ft per second. It leaves the barrel of the gun at a temperature of more than 330 degrees Celsius. That is 626 degrees Fahrenheit. Then on impact with the human skull the bullet would penetrate the skull causing vibration, shock waves, and a burning trail of damage that would destroy all in its path. Commonly, the bullet would not have the same force after its deceleration upon passing through the cooler human body fluids, to escape the skull. Instead, the bullet would then proceed to ricochet and destroy randomly all it encountered. The result for the victim of the gunshot would be quite dead. This was the fate of many of the men in the alley in Shepherds Pass on the night it all began. There had been a light drizzle all evening, but that drizzle had not interrupted anything anyone had planned. It was welcomed. The warm Missouri evenings of May sometimes make people long for the relief of a brief respite.

In the 1800s a group of cattlemen involved in feuding with the local sheep herders had blocked the main path to water and grassland from the herds of sheep. The sheepherders accepted that they were outnumbered and outgunned and devised a secret pass that would allow them a back door into the watering holes and the plentiful grassland. The secret area became known later as Shepherds Pass. No one at that time needed to put Shepherds Pass on a map, lest war break out. When Highway 70 was built, an off-ramp was constructed to allow people access to the ragged, dilapidated town that had now sprung up, because the town offered two very vital things the area needed. First, was a gas station that carried diesel fuel for the trucks that moved down the highway all night long. And two if offered two all-night tow and auto repair shops. The repair shops were owned by the Dodd brothers Leo and Raymond. As the country grew and its needs changed so did the needs and tastes of the Dodd brothers. They became involved in gambling and prostitution and bootlegging during the twenties. The sins of man rained and caused the off-the-road Truckstop to grow into a small town.

At some point, the two Dodd brothers chose different paths. Leo Dodd married and started a family that fought hard to legitimize the existence of the family businesses. Leo Dodd's offspring sought education and philanthropy. Leo Dodd's children and their children would spend years after his death struggling to cleanse the family name.

Raymond Dodd and his children went the other path entirely. They believed in the ways of organized crime and sought just as hard to excel in their felonious endeavors as the Children of Leo did in education and goodwill. Due to a common beginning and the view from spectators from the outside the family they were destined to always be an overlap in the family's values and name.

Chapter 2

Three men exited a shiny new rental car for a meeting with three other men. The first three men were led by a short stocky man chewing on a cigar that had long gone out. The stocky man carried a briefcase full of cash. You would not have to be told there was something of great value in the case, it was evident by the look on his face. The two men on his right and left were classic bodyguard types in shiny new suits. Their eyes focused straight ahead eyeing the group approaching. The group approaching looked like an almost mirror image of the first group. The short man in the center of the second group had no briefcase and his smile was even oilier than the simile of his counterpoint. "I hate Lawyers." The stocky man from the first group muttered almost to himself. Then he looked at the man on his right and then to the man on his left did I ever tell you guys about how much I hate lawyers." The first man's bodyguard grunted in harmony. "Once a lawyer screwed me so I ended up in the pen just so he could screw my wife at that time." his face contorted in a hideous remembrance. "I straighten that out when I got out, I only wish I could have killed them more than once." He chuckled in a deep baritone laugh. The meeting of the two groups was set for the alley behind a Chinese restaurant. The alleys in Shepherds Pass were remarkably clean. But the drizzle has started to loosen some other layers of ooze and sticky stuff found in alleys that no one is quite sure what it is or if they care to know. Shepherds Pass alleys were nothing like the alley in movies and on tv where there is an assortment of discards and derelicts, that seem to reach through the media you are watching and make you want a shower. With the mist and drizzle, the clean alley was even cleaner than usual. Light bounced off a red brick wall and laminated a spot where the corner of the building formed. Both groups of men walked toward the light. It was the natural place to conduct business on hand.

"This fucking blackmail." The speaker from the first group complained as the two groups converged under the light.

"It's greenmail and it's legal. Ask any lawyer."

"It's unethical as shit."

"So did you bring a priest or just the cash?"

There was a whistling undefinable sound not unlike a sworn of bees followed quickly by the dropping of two of the guards, one from each group. Another two guards fell and as the principals of the exchange turned to look toward the darkened area near the far corner, they had just enough time to make out two men emerging with the long barrel pistols. The two men emerged from the darkened corner toward the men under the light. The two last victims looked at each other in total disbelief. They had been so unprepared for a gun battle. And the direction from which the assault originated added insult to injury. In what seemed to be the final copulation the two last victims faced the shooters and did not even go for their guns, instead, they accepted the .22 long rifle bullets to their heads. And the damage was done; for now, they rested in the eternal sleep known as death.

Chapter 3

"Hey, Lavon," Wendell called out as Lavon got out of his raggedy pickup truck. The truck continued to click and pop, making a variety of cooling and adjusting noises long after it was turned off. Lavon Tyler was a newly assigned detective in Shepherds Pass.

But Lavon was no stranger to investigations. He had most recently been working for the Mississippi State Police. Lavon graduated from Florida State University where he played football before entering the military.

"Hey, right back at you, Wendell." Wendell Bishop and Lavon had only met earlier that day when Lavon was checking in, but they became fast friends, exchanging joking comments about the life of a police officer.

Bishop stood six foot two, a couple of inches shorter than Lavon. Officer Bishop had a lean tight muscle mass body that was like a sprinter or marathon runner. He was a black man with a cleanly shaven face and a business-like look about himself.

"Just like the circus" Wendell commented as Lavon walked closer.

A row of police cars stood lined up in various states of parking disarray, with their rooftop lights flashing. A line has been set for the crime scene and a boundary was being set for spectators and press.

"Reminds me more of a state fair," Lavon confessed as he walked closer. He could see a woman with dark curly hair that fell to her shoulders in a dark rumpled business suit kneeling over the bodies of several men.

There was an older man in a medical examiner's jacket examining the bodies. Lavon took a moment and stood observing.

"If you are looking for the cotton candy, we're all out." Wendell joked.

"Buddy, I need you to do a couple of things for me.

First, I need you to tape off that area over there by those dumpsters." Lavon's face suddenly looked like he was seeing something that others might be missing, as he pointed out the area to be sequestered. "Then I need you to get some strong lights. Cops usually don't have the best, so you might have to borrow from the fire department or the highway department. "Amazing" Lavon commented to himself.

"Anything, but what are we doing?"

"I need that area searched."

"Are we looking for anything in particular? You do know the bodies are over there. And by the way, that lady is your new partner, Abby Blackwell."

"Shell casings would be nice, but footprints may have to do.

And is she nice?"

"Who's footprints? And only in an alcoholic slutty way."

"Any footprints you can find. I need to know the number of pairs. And do you have firsthand knowledge of the slut thing?"

"No, I promised my Grandmother I would never swim in muddy water."

"Uniform, I want the press and spectators back behind the line." A tall gruff man who looked like the drill sergeant from dozens of army movies shouted as he walked up. The Sargent had stripes on his shoulder that told of his authority. Lavon turned to face the Sargent and stood toe to toe while staring back into his face.

"Sargent, I don't know what the rules are for socializing on the crime scene are here in Shepherds Pass, but I just gave this officer instructions to assist in the handling of this case." Lavon usually wore jeans and sports jackets. He wore running shoes because he loved to run or jog. He pushed back his jacket, revealing his badge and gun. The Sargent, whose name tag read "Rush" looked surprised at the badge. "Please don't tell me in my next report I will be writing about how the uniformed officers have a Sargent that will not allow them to find what looks like dangerous criminals."

"No, Sir." Rush strutted. "But Abby is the Detective in charge."

"And I am her partner."

"She did not say anything."

"She doesn't know yet. But I just saw the Lt show up and she will introduce us, then she will know, and we can all rejoice. In the meantime, will you let this man work? Because if that drizzle turns to rain, we will miss what we are looking for."

Chapter 4

"**D**etective Abby Blackwell, this is Detective Lavon Tyler. He is your new partner" Lt Crawford announced while Abby was still kneeling and working with the medical examiner. Abby looked over her shoulder at Lavon, then gave him a head-to-toe once over.

"Nice to meet you ma'am" Lavon offered his hand. It was as if he had offered her a dead lizard.

She looked at his hand, then turned back around ignoring him.

"I need a partner, so you go get Gomer Pyle what the fuck."

"What you need is to check that attitude if you need your job. The way I see it this is the biggest case to hit Shepherd in forever and it could pull your." Lt Crawford paused. "Fucked up career out of the shitter so yes this is your partner. He is an experienced detective, and we are short on people. Besides, not everyone wants to work with you or didn't you get the memo."

Abby looked down at the ground, sufficiently humiliated.

"So, Detective Blackwell. And I do use that term with caution. What do you think you have?" Lt Crawford asked. Crawford was a tough-looking woman who had, no doubt, earned her rank on the streets.

She wore concealer to conceal some of the lines the fifty-plus years of age had granted her, but it was the lines that showed through that best described her features and highlighted her face. She wore Ben

Franklin-style silver spectacles, resting on her short nose. The specs added an air of administration to the natural toughness.

"Well, I think we have drugs in Shepherd. I think this was a drug deal gone sideways. These three met in the alley with these three.

They argue and then gunplay breaks out and everyone is dead." Abby reported.

"Then you found drugs?" Lavon asked. Abby took a deep cleansing breath before answering.

"No, Cletus, I think the shooter grabbed the drugs and did a Carl Lewis, before we got here."

"Is that what you see, Lavon?" Crawford asked with obvious skepticism in her voice.

"No, not at all."

"Well please enlighten us with your minutes of observation, Homer." Abby spat at him.

"Lavon." He attempted to correct her.

"Same damn thing."

"Stand up and face me," Lavon instructed.

Reluctantly Abby stood up and gave Crawford a look that said if you were not here no way I would be doing whatever this is. Lavon put both hands on her shoulders.

"If I shot you and you were standing directly in front of me you would go flying backward." Lavon demonstrated with a little shove backward just enough for her to lose her balance and for him to catch her and help her regain equilibrium.

"Now if you were running forward and I shot you, you would meet the force of the bullet and drop in your tracks."

He stood staring in her face as if she should see his point.

"So." Lt Crawford smiled at the fact that Abby had missed Lavon's point.

"So that fat guy fell on that little guy who was on his right."

Abby stood blinking hoping she would catch up soon.

"Detective Blackwell there is no way that if I shot you standing in front of you, you would go flying sideways. It's against the laws of Mississippi physics and it probably is the same here."

Lt Crawford suppressed a chuckle and waited for Lavon to explain further. Lavon looked at Wendell who had been searching for tacks near the dumpster. Wendell looked up and smiled. Sargent Rush also looked up, but mostly in amazement. He was examining the area in front of the second set of dumpsters and had found something as well. Rush and Wendell seemed to be comparing notes and then started toward Lavon and the group to whom he was explaining his theory.

"Both sets of guys met under that light." Lavon points up at the streetlight. "When they got under the light someone came from over there and shot them. Which is amazing. They were using .22 caliber pistols."

"At that distance?" Abby interrupted looking at where Wendell and Rush had been examining.

Lt Crawford now looked sufficiently entertained.

"Continue Lavon."

The shock from Abby that the Lt had used called Lavon by his first name did not go unnoticed.

"I know Lavon's father; he was a police chief. Now he is a novelist." Lt attempted to repair the misspeak.

"Well, you won't find any drugs because no druggy is going to leave a suitcase full of money behind. Only a pro can shoot that well in the semidarkness. They would be using a .22 revolver, so even if we had the gun, we could not match the slug."

"He is right all the shots came from .22 or .25 caliber nothing as large as the guns these guys are carrying." The medical examiner, who had been working diligently to get the bodies out of the rain, finally weighed in.

"Two Guys," Rush reported as he met the group.

"How do you know two?" Abby asked.

"Because, as I am sure you would know, different men have different size body parts. The guy Officer Bishop found tracks for was a size 9 shoe. The guy over by the dumpster I checked was a 14 at least."

"Any Idea what the gait was on Big Foot," Lavon asked Rush.

"Gait?" Wendell asked.

"He's asking about the walking distance and pace. Also, the standing distance between the guy's feet.

It's a way to estimate how big an animal is that you are tracking." Rush answered in a tutoring tone. "Your Big Foot is over Six foot Six and weighs in at over two hundred fifty pounds. The other guy is about Bishop's height and weight."

"Like I said Blackwell, Lavon is a detective" Lt stated before making the most theatrical exit she could.

"Sorry partner I wasn't trying to show you up, but those guys are pros, and they won't be here long" Lavon stated to Abby who did not seem to care what he said next.

"Get your guy stopping rental cars with two passengers for an ID check. And Sargent no one I don't care if they have a hundred years on the job, no one stops those cars solo. Do you read me?"

"Loud and clear."

"I HAVE TO DEAL WITH sucks ups and kiss asses all my life, so, cowboy you are no different," Abby mumbled turning to walk away.

"I'm from Mississippi, not Texas, that makes me more Plowboy than Cowboy."

"Whatever, all I know is that right now I need a drink."

And with that, she was off. Lavon continued to work on the scene.

Chapter 5

At thirty-four years of age, Lavon only slept between 4 and 6 hours a night. Therefore, since he spent quite a bit of time at the crime scene and then went to the office to check messages and start a daily report, it did not seem much to him. Sargent Rush influenced the Missouri Highway Patrol and contacted them to try to stop the shooters from leaving the area. Rush gave regular reports to Lavon. Lavon also had officers sent to the train station airports to observe. But his instincts told him they were still here in Shepherds Pass. The instincts fell short of telling him where or even why, but he had a chilling feeling this was just the beginning, and he was afraid his partner was not up to the task.

"Sign this," Lavon asked Abby. Abby had come in late, and Lavon had chosen to give her time to acclimate. She looked hungover and her eyes registered a bad mood, but to press forward he could not wait any longer.

"I am not signing shit."

"Please, it's the daily report. This way it shows both of us working on this case."

"I don't do dailies."

"We need to."

"Why?"

"Because this case is going to get a lot of attention. That means the Lt is going to be constantly asking us questions to get her superiors off her back. The only way we get any peace to work the case is to stay in front of them."

Abby seemed to be genuinely thinking about what he had said. Lavon was not sure if she was considering his request or just the next country put down. She grabbed the report and signed it.

"Right now, I am trying to help us since we seem to be tethered."

Abby ran her hand through her oily curly hair and then looked at Lavon.

"I get it, so you are trying to help me."

Lavon sidestepped the comment and pulled the report she had worked on from the night before.

"You want the lab or the autopsy?"

"Well pass and pass. First, the fags in the lab hate me. But I guess they are going to love you in those tight-fitting jeans, she did her best Conway Twitty impersonation. Second, I puke anytime I go on the same floor as the autopsy."

"It's got to be done."

"I'll tell you what. Why don't I sit here and close out the crap I was working on before the gunfight at OK Corral and you get started on the new stuff."

"Fair enough," Lavon offered, a little happy that she was not accompanying him with her bad attitude in tow. The Shepherds Pass Police station at Tucker was in the process of being closed and moved to the new building that was still under construction, across the park from the current location. There were boxes of records with a system of color coding and notes taped to the storage boxes that defied human comprehension. Lavon hated autopsy more than anything else in police work. He had been raised in a large Christian family and sitting through the ultimate dismantling of the body challenged his resolve. Today he had to sit through not one be six. The only saving grace was that there were at least two always going on, so his time was shorted but he still felt sick to his stomach from the large doses of formaldehyde he had been inhaling. Lavon blamed his lightheadedness on missing pictures and prints and walked past that department several times before finding it until one of the clerks explained the sign had been taken down to be used at the new building.

"Where have you been?" A slender Blackman with heavy eye makeup and pink fingernails asked Lavon when he walked into the lab.

"I'm Detective Tyler."

"Of course, you are honey. Are you saying that, so you know who you are? They tell me there is a new Dick who feels the need to rush us around and there is one thing I know is new Dick when I see one."

"That's actually pretty funny." The lab was standard with technicians, who looked like high school kids who were angry with their parents for one reason or another. They were working feverishly on an assortment of things that could have been anything from curing cancer to the latest version of a pirated video game.

"Don't mind her she's such a Diva. She is just cranky because we have been left in the basement for too long and we're next to where they store dead bodies," A thin white guy with a space-age hairdo offered.

"I take it you found something." Lavon guessed.

"Of course, I did, but where is that ugly pit bull of a partner of yours?"

"Detective Blackwell is catching up with the other work we have. What did you find?"

"Did you want to go and find someone to explain it to you?"

Lavon looked back at the Black Technician not sure what his response was supposed to be. "Look if you promise to speak slowly and try not to use too many big words, I will do my best to follow. If I don't understand, I will ask questions or find someone who can explain."

"Fair enough, by the way, I am Aaron." Lavon reached over to shake the technician's hand, but Aaron offered his hand as if it was to be kissed. Lavon chose to bypass the kiss.

"There was three million dollars. Sequential and still in packs. The only prints there will be from bank employees."

"So, there is nothing?" Lavon concluded.

"Hold on cowboy keep it in your pants." As soon as Aaron's statement hit the air one of the other lab technicians yelled out "I bet that's the first time you ever said that."

Lavon laughed but was now curious.

"I sent a print to pictures and prints, it's in the folder you are carrying."

"So, there was a print in the suitcase?" Lavon sought to clarify.

"No, the suitcase had been wiped clean but there were a couple of partials. I reconstructed the partials and created a print that the system will allow. You got a hit. But the big problem is that it's a print to me, but creative art in a court of law. You must duck the fruit of the poison tree. Which means...."

"I can't use the print as evidence, only as a general jump-off point or some smart lawyer sinks the case," Lavon added.

"Cute and smart too. Maybe you should leave your partner upstairs from now on."

Lavon turned to walk away and stopped at the door. "Hey, you guys like pizza?"

"Don't play with me, cowboy. I love pizza." Aaron answered.

"Well, I am going to the pizza place next to the Chinese restaurant where the guys got killed, and to break the ice with them, why don't I order pizza for you guys."

"Bless you."

"Thank you, I appreciate the help."

WHEN LAVON RETURNED to the squad room, he could feel the difference in the atmosphere. There was heat now. People had a look that told him they were minding their own business and did not want to be involved in anything transpiring around them. His first notion was that it was him. But as he got closer, he knew better. Abby was in a corner arguing with a tall muscular man who looked more like a movie star than anyone you would run into in a police station. The man had perfect dark wavy hair and a capped smile even though it was clear he was enjoying watching Abby squirm.

"Mount up Detective Blackwell, we got interviews to do if we are going to get out of here at a decent time tonight" Lavon lofted on the air to free Abby from whatever it was she was engaged in. It did not look good for her.

"Yeah, let me get my purse." She answered.

The man she had been speaking to clearly did not like the disruption. He turned to look at Lavon with a look that measured and sized him up and, in the assessment, found him lacking. "You must be the new cowboy who caught a piece of the hot case?" Lavon could see now the man was wearing a badge that resembled his.

"Plowboy, not Cowboy. It's Mississippi, not Texas."

"A shit kicker by any other name." He walked closer to Lavon in a deliberate attempt to intimidate him.

"Lucas Howard, Detective."

"Lavon Tyler, shitkicker."

"Luck of the draw you got the hot case. Try not to fuck it up too much before someone realizes you and sugar tits are over your heads."

Howard was sending off all types of alarm bells for Lavon. Lavon had six brothers and his father was a cop when he was young. The Tyler boys had decided that no one was going to victimize any of their sisters. That did not mean everything was always peaceful, but it meant that the safety of their sisters came before any petty squabbles. It also was agreed that some matters had to be solved and dad or mom was never to be told to preserve the bond. There was Lucas, not only attempting to bully Lavon but harassing Abby. Lucas leaned forward so only Lavon could hear and whisper. "I know you probably want to look like a big man and get a little of that ass. And that's cool, but keep in mind, I am the alpha male here and when I want it back, I will come and get it and you just get out of the way or roll over."

"Tyler, let's do those interviews." Abby had returned and she was not clear what she was seeing Lavon in or Lucas's faces, but it was clear there was trouble brewing.

"Detective Tyler, there is a heavy-weight boxing qualifier tonight at six in the main gym. It's for the fire department vs the police department charity at the end of the year. I need a spar. If you aren't too busy, why don't you strap on a pair of gloves and if necessary, a pair of balls and get in the ring with me? You might learn a few things about yourself" Howard yelled across the squad room as Abby and Lavon were leaving.

"Don't fight him it's a setup."

"I know."

Lt Crawford insisted Lavon check out a vehicle from the motor pool. She was not happy with him arriving in a rusted-out, beat-up truck. Since Abby knew the area better than he Lavon allowed her to drive, but felt he may have made a mistake in that she seemed shaky.

"You don't know him, and you don't owe anybody anything. Hell, I don't even think you like me so why would you set your set yourself up to be mangled by that nut case?"

"Did you check the results I brought back from the autopsy and the labs?" Lavon asked. Jason Ivy, Morris Tanner, and Gordon Fisher were team one and Ken Mallard, Joe Bushman, and Clark Peterson make up the second team."

"Is this your way of saying you are changing the subject?" They proceeded to drive and there was silence. First, they interview the people at the pizza restaurant, Salvatore's. The staff had seen nothing, and many had been there the night of the killing and had joined the spectators but were clearly in the dark as to what had happened. They were, however, grateful to have Lavon's order for pizza delivery to the police lab basement. The next group interviewed were the Chinese restaurant employees at Kaloowan Restaurant. No one had seen anything, but they did remember emptying used grease from the fryers into the bins in the back. The grease is collected and sold as part of the soap-making process. The bins leak and that is what helped cause the footprints. In the field, Lavon noticed Abby worked well. She was good with young kids and often knew questions to ask that had escaped him. There was still a bit of volatility in her, as proven with they went to the Loop Bar. The Loop Bar was one of the businesses facing the man-made lake where many Shepherds Pass businesses were located. There was a huge pedestrian bridge in the middle of the lake leading to the hotel and housing side of the area.

"I stay over there," Lavon announced as he noticed Abby staring at the water.

"Enjoy it while you can. All those old hotels are being bulldozed for new chain hotels. Dodd family on the move."

Lavon explained about the partial fingerprint. It belonged to Amber Dodd, the chief financial officer for Middle West Investments. The dead man that had been carrying the suitcase full of money, Joe Bushman, showed as an employee of Middle West Investments. They decided to make it their last stop for the day. The lobby of Middle West Investments reeked of opulence. There were giant vases and a waterfall with koi. There was a thick pile carpet and Asian lanterns hung. The staff were dressed immaculately, and they all looked like they had just stepped out of Hollywood casting. A woman in a Silk dress with an Asian collar came over after the third secretary that had sent Lavon and Abby in various directions.

"I am Ruth, I am Ms. Dodd's personal assistance, and perhaps there is something I can help you with officer." She spoke directly to Lavon as if Abby was not there. It was clear that it bothered Abby, but she did not let it show, instead letting it build.

"Tell her it's about a dead friend of hers and a big bag of money that I don't quite know what to do with."

Ruth looked terrified and scurried away.

"That was bad," Abby observed.

"Look who's talking."

Amber Dodd entered the room and took over. Her presence sucked all the randomness of stray attention and drew it to a focal point. She sashayed in wearing a clinging red dress that accented every aspect of the femininity she possessed. Her dress was low cut, daring her breasts to break free and make an appearance. She wore matching red alligator pumps and large gold bracelets and a necklace. She was being followed by an Asian woman in a kimono. "Shame on you for shocking my assistant." Amber offered with a smile. She had a beautiful face that was the combination of expensive surgeries and the best of cosmetics. With a hairdo that told that she frequented the best salons.

"Can I have Kai bring you anything, coffee tea, or perhaps something stronger, it is getting a little late." Amber offered in the most cordial tone.

"Nothing for me, thank you" Lavon answered. Abby looked at the stocked bar but said nothing. The office was sunken with deep carpeting and overstuffed leather sofas. There was a conference table with chairs for ten in one corner of the room that overlooked the lake. Amber led them to the sofa and seated them. She sat close to Lavon and leaned forward, almost touching him.

"I am Detective Tyler, and this is my partner, Detective Blackwell."

"Yes, I know the University of Florida Seminole football" Amber sounded genuine in her praise.

Lavon was concerned that Amber had been given a heads-up and had had time to research her investigators. Amber leaned close to Lavon. "How can I help you two?"

"Joe Bushman. Was he working for you last night?" Lavon asked.

"Let's say hypothetically he was, does that make me a suspect?" Amber asked.

"No wrong shoe size," Lavon answered.

"Was he delivering a blackmail payment?" Abby asked.

"No" answered Amber.

Lavon was aware her answer to Abby's questions was short.

"It was Greenmail, wasn't it?" Lavon asked.

"Damn, the luck. I get the one smart cop in the force."

"By the way that is a wonderful perfume you are wearing."

Amber leaned closer. "It's a custom fragrance. Made just for me, but to get the full effect you must smell it up close. She leaned close, offering him her neck and allowing him the full view of her cleavage. Then she looked at Abby and rolled her eyes.

He was more than an employee; he was a friend of the family from the old days."

"How is the mayor taking it," Abby asked.

Lavon was not sure what that meant but he did not mind waiting to find out.

"You can ask him." Amber stood and walked over to the bar and poured a tumbler of whiskey then walked back and sat the glass on the office desk.

"I was wondering if we can help each other." Lavon offered. Amber walked over to admire the view of the lake. "What do you have in mind, I don't do threesomes." She looked back over her shoulder at Abby.

"Well, I have this problem. I have a big box of money on the floor at the foot of my desk. The damned thing is in the way. Now a big move and construction is going on and I would hate that box of money to get misplaced. I also think a box such as that is bad to have around even good cops if you get my drift."

"I see your problem; how can I help?"

"Let's say the owner of the money sits down with their legal representative and makes out a statement expressing that the money is theirs and was in the possession of an employee."

"I think I see where you are going. That way no one is spending time investing in anything legal."

"I think you see my point because your shareholders don't want to hear about greenmail and money in my office doesn't earn interest."

"So, what would I owe you," Amber asked turning around and noticing the glass of whiskey was now half full. Lavon noticed it also but neither spoke of it and Abby sat there wordless.

LAVON TRIED HIS BEST to be silent for the drive back, but he could not. "What the hell was that?"

"What? "Abby tried faking innocence.

"Look if you as much as make a half-ass attempt to help yourself, I'm all there. But you can't live like this disrespecting yourself." Lavon never thought he would find himself preaching but it was all he had.

"Look, you aren't perfect. I say you were looking at those fake tits."

"I think you are better than this Abby. If I am wrong just tell me." Lavon closed with that; he said no more for the ride back to the station. It was time to put his mind in the right frame for the boxing match.

Chapter 6

Word had no doubt gone out and the police gym was standing room only. Lavon knew pounding a new guy was probably par for the course for Lucas and everyone wanted to come and watch the train wreck. Today, it was going to be a wreck of a different type they would witness. Having boxed golden gloves, Lavon knew he felt most comfortable in a packed room full of strangers. No one to please. No one to apologize to for what he was going to do. Wendell came to work his corner, but they had said little in the way of words, but much him the way of closeness.

"It's not too late to back out Lavon you got my respect." Wendell offered. Lavon stood in his corner facing Wendell praying silently to himself. Hoping God would understand some men are born to stop those that destroy the lives of others.

"Hey, shit kicker I am going to pull your pants down and spank you just to let everyone know who the alpha is around here." Lucas had walked up behind Lavon and was trying to break his concentration as he prayed. Booker, a big Blackman who oversaw much of the cadet training came up to usher Lucas back to his corner. "Walk back kid, it's only a qualifier."

"This guy says he is good to go to let the leather fly, so why do we give the house a real show, Booker?"

"Alright by me if you clowns want to do the dance for real, but keep in mind both corners have the right to throw in the towel," Booker announced.

"My Girl Nya is in the audience. I want you to meet her later." Wendell stated to Lavon who might as well have been a statue with the degree of focus he entranced.

When the bell for round one rang both men tapped gloves and Lavon started his footwork. Lucas shook his head, smiled at the crowd then walked straight in. Lucas swung a big right hand but missed and opened his right side for a left and right combination by Lavon that snapped the head of Lucas back and shot sweat and water from his head. The crowd roared and jumped to its feet. This was happening. Lucas barreled forward to tie Lavon up to push him into a corner to work him over, but Lavon slid to the right and threw a left hook to the body followed by another right to the same one of Lucas's eyes. The same eye he had been working from the beginning. Lucas's eye was swollen, and it was clear he could not see through it. Lavon threw a series of left and right to Lucas's head, so Lucas had no choice but to raise his gloves to cover. Lavon began slamming Lucas's body pounding rights and lefts that seemed to almost lift him off his feet. Lavon threw Lucas into a corner and began pounding him. Lucas dropped to one knee just as the bell rang. Wendell began sponging Lavon, but Lavon did not take the stool he stood staring at Lucas. When bell two rang Lavon ran to Lucas's corner and started pounding him almost before he could get up from the stool. A big right hand landed on Lucas's jaw, and he dropped onto the mat. Booker ran over, but Lavon would not step back, so the count of ten could not start. Lavon wanted him to get up for more of the beating.

"Look Detective I'm not fucking with you, get back this aint that kind of fight," Booker screamed into Lavon's face then turned to Lucas's corner. "Did you motherfuckers lose your towel?"

One of the men in Lucas's corner said. "He said no towel, let the shit fly." By this time Lucas was on his feet again and he was wobbly and dazed. Lavon started hitting him again and the bell rang.

"Please don't kill him, Lavon. Whatever the demon is that ran you out of your life in the south, it won't be put back right by killing Lucas" Wendell begged Lavon. When bell three rang Lavon cornered Lucas. Lavon spits out his mouthpiece. "You are going to apologize to her and Wendell or right here and right now I am going to show everyone who the bitch is because I am going to pull your pants down." Lucas nodded his head in agreement and then, for good measure, Lavon knocked him out.

Chapter 7

"So, Nya, this big dumb country boy is Lavon. We must be nice to him because he is homesick and most of the people here treat him like shit" Wendell introduced as a large group had gathered after the boxing preliminaries in Patrick's, one of the bars, that faced the lake on the far end. Cops, Firemen, and hospital personnel loved this bar because it served breakfast, lunch, or dinner at any hour that it was open. Nya took Lavon's hand and began examining.

"What is she doing Wendell?" Wendell took another swig of his beer before answering. "She is reading your palm. Her mother is some kind of Cajun Queen in the swamps somewhere and Nya reads people sometimes." Nya had smooth black skin and large eyes. She had a smile that easily lit up any room.

"It is still there."

"What," Lavon asked, not sure he wanted her to answer.

"The pain and the embarrassment." For a moment Nya and Lavon locked eyes.

"Relax, big guy, she is never going to say anything she read that will hurt someone's feeling in front of people." Wendell offered. The bar was filled, and yet, somehow more and more people packed in. People were drinking and socializing out in front of the bar.

"No offense Nya but I don't know if I believe in that voodoo stuff." Nya seemed to ignore Lavon's comment.

"Take her with you." Sargent Rush entered the bar with a group of equally fit men of his age group. "Hey Bishop, why didn't you tell me your friend is a boxer." The shift of the crowd seemed to make people lose track of people and Lavon was not sure if Nya had answered his last questions. Lavon wandered over to the bridge to the motel where he was staying alone.

Chapter 8

"**B**ooty Call." Lavon had been catapulted out of a sound sleep. Now a drunken woman was banging on a door in the motel, yelling obscenities at anyone trying to quit her. "Booty Call." Lavon was now awake enough to realize it was his door that was being banged on. Lavon "Though what kind of idiot would bang on the door of a cop at 3:00 in the morning." It was Abby. Lavon sprang across the room not even noticing, he was wearing only his boxers as he did on hot nights. He opened the door and Abby stood there swaying leaning on the door jamb for balance.

"Good, you're ready." She assessed, eyeing Lavon's current state of undress. Abby hobbled past Lavon, not to mention that she was only wearing one shoe. She threw her purse on the bed and proclaimed, 'Let the fucking begin." Abby kicked off her remaining shoe and began struggling to pull her dress off over her head. Lavon struggled with her, trying to stop her.

"Abby I am not going to have sex with you."

She looked at him. "Why not? You won." Lavon motioned her to the bed.

"Why don't we talk about it after you rest." Moments later, Abby was sound asleep. Lavon sat in the only chair in the room, studying her, and watching her sleep. There was something he had realized in his dream about the case. Now awake, he struggles to recapture it. What had he missed?

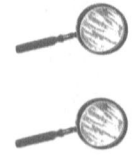

"GEE, I GUESS I FUCKED up big time. You didn't even have the courtesy to fuck me so you could feel as bad as I do." Abby had popped awake after noticing the sun was now peering through gaps in the cheap, mass-produced curtains of the motel. Lavon sat in the chair with his back to her, thinking and scribbling. "This is the part where you say something," Abby informed him.

"I went for a run earlier and I brought back coffee and rolls, they are over on the dresser." Abby got a coffee and rolls.

"So, is this how it's going to work? The shittier I treat you the better you treat me" There was no immediate response "Look, we need to talk." Lavon kept looking away. "I love alcohol. I have for as long as I can remember. When I was a kid, alcohol was my best friend. I was ugly and clumsy and stupid, but alcohol didn't seem to care. I was shy, but I found with my friend alcohol, I could be the life of the party. And then when I realized what a fuck up I was alcohol consoled me. I tried AA but in a small town everyone knows everyone, so you don't dare share. I walked in with my head held high. Now I want to find a group somewhere where no one knows me and crawl in with my tail between my legs." The Abby confessing hardly resembled the brass smart-ass cop Lavon met in the alley only a night before. "I'm not asking you to feel sorry for me. All I want is a chance. I know you are smart and smart; since you put Lucas in the hospital, you are probably thinking you could get his partner and throw me on the scrap heap." Lavon had not considered asking for a partner switch but there was a certain logic to what she was saying. "In that alley, you saw everything I missed and would have taken me days to correct." Lavon finally turned to look at her. "Abby I am not strong enough to watch you self-destruct. If you promise you will try even a little, then we can work together."

"Deal, what's next?"

"Well, we need to check in at the station, then we have a car rental company to visit."

"You shouldn't rent one, you should buy one. And I can help you find a place to burn the pile of shit truck you drove into town." Lavon gave her a look of total consternation.

Oh sorry, old habits die hard." She slurped her coffee and went for another roll.

Chapter 9

"**A**re you an idiot or is this your idea of a practical joke?" Judge Lynn Masterson sneered at Lavon in her chambers. Lavon had taken Abby to freshen up then went to the station to complete the daily report. Before he could turn it in, Lt Crawford jumped him for being reckless and caused her to be down a Detective. In exchange for the daily report, she handed him the papers to have the money from the alley returned to the owners. This meant a trip to the District Attorney's office which Lavon got lost trying to find. Then the clerk in the District Attorney's office told him he needed a signature from a judge and recommended Judge Masterson. Now, he stood in front of Judge Masterson. Masterson was beautiful in Lavon's eyes, and he struggled not to stare. She read the request and asked him to join her in her chambers. They were joined by Terrell, a huge Black officer in a brown uniform who looked like a football nose tackle.

"Ma'am, if you could tell me what part of this makes you upset, I could maybe look into it." Judge Masterson has short, curly, blond hair, and piercing brown eyes. She looked like someone he had seen recently, but he could not put his finger on who. She stared at him, clearly wondering if he was joking.

"First off, you can drop that bumpkin accent. You don't do it well. Second, I know who all the detectives are and there is no Detective Tyler." Lavon cleared his throat and looked at Terrell who might as well have been a stone statue of Terrell.

"Well, judge I am from Lamont, Mississippi, and anyone there would say you people have the accent. And secondly, I can show you my driver's license and birth certificate, and if need be, I could bring in my mom and dad to prove I do exist." Lavon looked at Terrell. "I have only been in town a couple of days but is that non existing people a real big problem here?" Judge Masterson hung her head forward and when she raised it, she was laughing. "Terrell take this across the hall and get it signed." She handed the request to Terrell, and he looked at Lavon. "He'll be fine here, Terrell." After Terrell left chambers, Judge Masterson looked even more attractive to Lavon. "Look I apologize for insulting your accent. I had no way of knowing there was a new detective in town." Lavon smiled and stood at a loss for what to say or do. He was still hurting from the breakup that led him here. "I tell you what detective why I don't take you to lunch? I will meet you at the Warf at noon." Lavon was confused, did he just get asked out by a judge or was this professional courtesy?

LAVON AND ABBY WALKED up to the counter of the car rental agency. " The man behind the counter was tall and pale with a large Adam's apple and wore a bow tie. "Yes, these looks familiar, and that one is Joe, I know him well he rents cars for clients all the time and he is my go-to guy at Middle West Investments to get reimbursed for their clients trashing our cars." Lavon had handed him pictures of the men killed behind the Chinese restaurant. "Your go-to guy crossed over to the happy hunting ground," Abby informed him. "That is sad, you know for a thug, he was a nice guy." There was the twinge again that Lavon had experienced earlier. Thugs and investment brokers, what an unlikely pair, but they were a part of what was bothering him in his sleep. "Do you remember renting a vehicle to two men one about average height and the other very tall and broad like a mountain man?" Lavon asked, expecting a negative response.

"Oh, yeah. Those two clowns" Bowtie responded. "We are the only car rental company in town, so we have to rent to anyone, or we risk suits for discrimination." Lavon and Abby looked at each other and then back to Bowtie. "The shorter one was harassing women big time. he slapped an eighty-year-old woman on the ass and yelled come on grandma, let's get that motor started." Abby looked shocked. "Did you guys report it to the police?" Lavon asked. "Yes, and nothing happened." Lavon smiled. "I bet it did."

Chapter 10

"TELL ME AGAIN WHY ARE we doing this other than tempting the allergy gods," Abby asked. Lavon and Abby had returned to the station and Lavon had nuisance reports pulled by street officers working the area of the car rental agency. Bundles and boxes were covering the floor. "The guys we are looking for are on the surveillance cameras for the car rental. You find the day and a possible and we have a photo of our shooters. We then go to the local hotels and, presto, we got pictures."

"And we are going through all these boxes?" Abby asked, looking at the pile.

"Well, actually, I have a lunch date with a judge, so it looks like you get the start."

"In other words, you won't screw me one way, but you will screw me this way," Abby muttered as Lavon exited.

"YOUR DATE IS OVER THERE." A thin waitress greeted Lavon as he entered the Warf Seafood restaurant. It was barely noon, but the judge was already there. He had chosen a table with a view of the lake and the bridge. The table she had selected was big enough for six people or more, but she had covered the table with papers she was viewing and reviewing. Judge Masterson had a glass of tea in front of her and did not seem to acknowledge Lavon as he approached.

"My name is Robin, and I will be your server, what would you like to drink?" Lavon had noticed that Robin had taken him by the arm leading him to the table. When she asked for his order, her hand ran down his back. Lavon turned quickly, more in startlement than in offense, and at that exact moment, Judge Masterson chose to look up.

"Thank you" was the only comment Lavon could muster as Robin brushed by him, walking away. Lavon's heart sank as he looked down at the mountain of paperwork. Who was he to think this beautiful and smart woman would be interested in a down-home country boy?

"This place is quite good. Order whatever you like" Judge Masterson suggested. The air has started to fill with the sweet smell of ozone and impending rain. The smell was so sweet you couldn't seem to breathe it in fast enough. "Who's your partner?" Masterson asked.

" Abby Blackwell." Masterson looked at Lavon with a look of disdain.

"Watch your back." Lavon had been a policeman long enough to know not to pursue the statement. In a moment Robin appeared with their order and, it appeared that some of the buttons on her blouse had come unbuttoned as she leaned forward while collecting Lavon's menu. "I guess you get that a lot," Masterson said after failed attempts to ignore the serious flirting by the waitress.

"What?" Masterson put her pen down and stared at Lavon.

"Young girls throwing themselves at you."

"I don't think she is throwing herself at me. I think she thinks this is a business lunch not a date and she is trying to play to me for a bigger tip."

"Why would she not think this is a real date? As you say."

"To be honest, if this was a real date and my date had this much paperwork scattered on the table, it would be a signal that we did not have a relationship worth salvaging." Lavon knew it was cold and direct before he finished it. He knew you cannot be a cop and smart off to judges, but it was in the air and could not be called back. Judge Masterson stared at Lavon as no one had ever talked to her that way before. Robin, the waitress, sat on a bar stool and crossed her legs, allowing her skirt to rise to a dangerous level, while she counted receipts. It was not Robin's legs but the ring on Judge Masterson's finger that transfixed Lavon.

"I am widowed."

"I am sorry to hear that."

"The ring seems to cause you so much stress. Especially considering that girl is trying to get you to look at her underpants." Before Lavon could respond, his phone went off. Considering all the paperwork on the table, he had no compunction about answering.

"Detective Tyler."

"Hey, Sherlock, we got the guys. I ran the pictures through recognition and got an immediate hit. The FBI called the Lt, and they are on the phone now. The big guy is Monroe Ford, his record reads like a book on how to be a fuck-up. The other guy is Antonio Ramiro, a freak in general." it was Abby reporting much sooner than he thought.

"Get pictures off to the uniforms. Be sure to advise these guys are stone-cold killers, nobody approaches without our call. See if we can borrow Wendell and have him check the hotel."

"Let's get these guys." And Abby was off the phone.

Judge Masterson scribbled something on a piece of paper and handed it to Lavon. "This is my address. I owe you another apology and a real date. Come at six and we can have dinner." Judge Masterson looked genuinely apologetic. Lavon smiled. "Look it sounds like your case is heating up. You have got to go save the world. Besides, if you stay too much longer Robin over there is going to do a strip, compete with feathers." Lavon was not sure how he detected it, but he was sure there was a note of jealousy in her voice.

"HEY, LAVON. I MEAN Detective Tyler; I got your boys or at least their hotel. They are at the Drake. I am parked near the back, where they cannot spot me, and we have Officer Webber out front, and we are waiting for your arrival. Good luck" Wendell reported over the radio as Lavon and Abby sped to the scene. "You aren't wearing your vest, Lavon commented."

"I don't like wearing that thing, it chafes my nipples."

"Then invest in some nipple cream or shave or whatever it takes. But we back each other up properly or you stay in the car." It was the most forceful Abby had seen Lavon. It wasn't the cop in him; it was his military training.

"Roger that. By the way what is up with you and the Judge?"

"She wanted to apologize for calling me a bumpkin."

"You know it's the fucking truck. Burn it."

"I have a better truck. I lent it to Noreen."

"Is Noreen your girlfriend back in Hog Hollow?"

"No, she's my younger sister and she is in college to be a lawyer. Don't want her to miss a day. She might have to represent me for killing a partner." They both smiled at Lavon's joke. Maybe they had reached the point where put-downs and smart-mouth comments were about humor and not about going for the throat.

Chapter 11

In the lobby of the Drake Hotel, Lavon and Abby walked to the front desk clerk and showed him the picture of the two men they were looking for. "Oh yeah, Fick and Frack. That's what we call them."

"Why is that?" Abby asked.

"You know you don't see one without seeing the other."

"Are they in their rooms or do you have any idea when they will be back?" Lavon asked.

The receptionist at the desk was a young black girl with natural hair. She had a complexion that reminded Lavon of Nya, Wendell's girlfriend. A relative he thought.

"You're joking right, there're right there." The receptionist pointed and Antonio Ramiro was standing in the lobby waiting for the elevator. When the receptionist pointed, he saw her and drew his gun. His gun fired the whistling sound twice. Lavon grabbed Abby and barely managed to pull her out of the line of one of the shots. It whistled so close to her head that it made her hair fluff. The second shot went center mass into her chest. Luckily, she had worn the vest they had argued over. Not lucky for the receptionist as the first bullet went into her forehead so quickly the surprised look on her face frozen for posterity. Abby fired three shots and all three hit Ramiro in the chest. He flew backward, falling into eternity. Lavon spotted Big Foot, Monroe Ford. Big Foot pulled his gun. Lavon shot the light fixture above Big Foot's head and a host of light and electric sparks shot off.

Everyone in the lobby that was not running and praying was now doing so. Some of the guests may have missed the hiss of the twenty-two or even Abby's response, but the light show with electric sparks could not be overlooked. Lavon's miss had been deliberate to drive Big Foot outside. Cops don't like gunfights in crowded lobbies. Big Foot ran with the former Seminole football player in hot pursuit. Lavon's biggest fear was that this assassination team had proven they were far better than the average person at shooting while running. If Big Foot turned around and shot, he might have to take the shot and hope it hit his vest to save anyone that did not clear the lobby or the exit way where they were headed. As Big Foot burst into the light of day, Webber a young dark-haired female uniform cop, was just getting out of the car to control the rush of people leaving the hotel. She went for her weapon and Big Foot shot her twice. Lavon had to choose, help the cop, or chase Big Foot, who was now running for the bridge. For Lavon, there was no choice.

"You caught one in the clavicle, and it looks broken. The other is in the chest, but your vest caught that. It's going to hurt like bitch, but no early retirement for you little lady" Lavon said as he pulled Webber's hand radio. Lavon started calling for officers to block off the south end of the bridge and for paramedics to arrive as soon as possible. He also ordered the coroners and a sergeant to block off the scene and collect all witnesses. As Lavon was applying pressure to Webber to help her blood clot, she looked at him. " Hey farm boy, I saw you fight the other night."

"What did you think?"

"God, I am so glad you kicked his ass. It isn't bad enough that he says demeaning things and feels you up, but it's like he campaigns for the other guys to join the, be a pig party."

"Does that mean you owe me a beer?"

"Anything Detective Tyler."

When Lavon reentered the lobby, a middle-aged woman was kneeling on the floor holding the hand of the receptionist." "She won't let go and we need to clear the area. It's a crime scene now. One uniform officer informed him. Lavon sat on the floor across from the woman with the deceased between them. He took the receptionist by the hand and looked at the woman. Then he said the Lord's Prayer. When Abby and Lavon exited the hotel, the woman that had helped send off the receptionist was clinging to Lavon crying. The local news could not get enough pictures of the image.

Chapter 12

"Oh, my Tyler, you poor man." A short stocky, middle-aged woman with a heavy Hispanic accent rushed Lavon as the door opened to the address that Judge Masterson had given him. The woman wore a pristine maid uniform and had tears in her eyes. Lavon had gotten lost twice trying to find the address to the secure, gated neighborhood. The house was white stone with large arched windows, marble stairs in front, and red wrought iron railing accentuating the look.

"Now just a moment. I decided to have you here to get you away all to myself and now I see Rosa molesting you." Masterson had appeared and saw Rosa holding Lavon.

"I no molest. You don't watch the local tv news because you say it can hurt what you do in court. But Mr. Tyler has been on the news all day. He saved his partner's life and lead a prayer for an innocent victim caught in a crossfire." Judge Masterson had done a total transformation. She now looked sexy in a sleek blue dress that accentuated her large breasts and clung to the contours of her butt. The dress was sleeveless and showed that peek-a-boo effect of her breasts as she moved.

"Wow," Lavon said as he took in the full effect of her changeover. She walked up to him and accepted the wine he had in his hand and kissed him lightly on the lips. "That is just clear up any misunderstanding of what this evening is about." Rosa stood blushing, then realized she was not needed at this time and vanished. "You know, I almost feel like you lied to me."

"How, so?"

"Well, I thought you were the type of cop who delivers subpoenas. And maybe rescues a cat or two out of a tree."

"Well. I caught multiple homicides the first night I hit town. I guess they were all out of cat cases, Judge."

"No. Here we are in private you must call me Lynn and I will call you Lavon. Now let's eat."

After dinner, they sat in a reception room that looked bigger than the entire first floor of the motel where Lavon was staying. Lavon sat staring at his wine glass with a look on his face that said he had something to say. "Okay. so, spit it out" Lynn Masterson finally asked.

It took a little time, but Lynn was patient as Lavon sought to find the words. "A few months back, I was in a relationship that ended leaving me feeling hurt and stupid. It's the main reason for my relocation. I don't ever want anyone to feel what I felt." Lavon paused, still looking at the swirl of the wine.

"So, you are apologizing for not being a love'em and leave'em kind of guy." Lynn waited to be sure she had his complete attention.

"When my husband died, part of me died. I have had a few dates in the years since but for the most part, I stay a prisoner locked in this grand palace. You come along and you seem free. Help me to be free." Lynn's brown eyes shined at Lavon, reflecting the child within trying to find the way out. "I was so jealous of the waitress today wanting to show you her underpants, I went out and bought sexy underwear myself on the off chance you might peek at them tonight."

"Maybe I should take a peek."

Lynn stood in front of Lavon, and he slowly raised the front of her dress.

"Wow."

"Wow is good right Lavon."

"Wow is outstanding."

"In that case let me give you a better look." And she unfastened the dress and let it drop to the floor then kicked it away."

They made love on the sofa like two people missing part of their existence and now knew how to fill the void. They proceeded to the bedroom to make mad, passionate, trusting love like lovers of old. Then, later that night they pressed, the bounds of lovemaking like two people with a thirst being filled from a deep well, knowing this well they must plan to visit often.

Lynn reached her naked body over Lavon's to get her glass from the nightstand on the side of the bed where he lay. Her genital region brushed his beneath the satin sheet and she wiggled a little to get the glasses. Lavon's genital region responded in a big way. "Again, Lavon. Look at this bed, it's sopping wet. How do you just know every button to press?" Lavon smiled and put his arm around her.

"Alright mister it's time for ground rules" Lynn announced.

"Rule one. If we are sleeping together for one week or one hundred years, it is monogamous. No sex on the side." Lavon started and Lynn rolled off him and looked up at the ceiling.

"That was going to be my rule one. Okay, I recuse myself from any case you are on and if your name shows up. That way, no one says you screwed me to get a good verdict."

"You have to respect that I cannot talk about open cases."

"That sounds more than fair. By the way, where are you staying."

"The Deluxe."

"That's a shit hole."

"Yeah, but I call it home."

"Get a house."

"I haven't had time to look for one, remember the statement about the shortage of cats in tree cases? I've been working on a real case since I got out of my truck."

"I can buy you one."

"I'll pretend you didn't suggest that."

"Why don't you help me find something? And I buy it."

"Sure, but I won't look at anything in the lower eighteens."

"What is that."

"That's right you aren't from here. The low rent lower end houses, not viewing the lake or on streets with numbers one through eighteen. Eighteen through nine is not bad but anything below ninth street is rough."

"Are there motels there?" Lavon got a thought shooting through his head.

"Yeah, if you are looking for hookers and drugs."

Chapter 13

Lavon entered the squad room with a new lease on life and feeling refreshed after his time with Lynn. He still had images when she slept of Nya's face superimposed over the face of the girl that was shot in the head at the Drake. But he had been a cop long enough to know most days you limit the bad in hopes of taking advantage of the good. He could see there were several men he did not know in the office of the Lt, and they seemed to be having a heated discussion.

"We are needed in the principal's office." Abby appeared behind him. She now looked even less like the mouthy party girl cop he met only a couple of days ago. She wore a dress shirt and had removed her suit jacket. The shirt was saturated in sweat. Her curly dark hair was matted with sweat and clumps of whatever she had been using to try and get it under control. Dark circles, the kind caused by lack of sleep, lined the bottom of her eyes. Abby grabbed Lavon by the arm and shoved him to a corner clearly, trying to get a moment of privacy to discuss something.

"I went to an AA meeting last night."

"Good."

"Look I got a sponsor, a rough former biker chick."

"How are you doing?"

"I got the sweats. Diarrhea and dizziness but other than that, I feel really shitty."

"But you are trying, that was the agreement."

"Look fucking Tom Sawyer, for new people in AA, sponsors usually recommended 30 and 30. That is thirty meetings in thirty days. My sponsor is old school, so for relapse people, she recommends 90 and 90. That is ninety meetings in ninety days. She also says that many alcoholics bolster and replace their emotions with booze. So, she is calling for ninety days with no new relationships. That includes ninety days with no sex. I passed out when she said it and had to be revived."

Lavon looked at her, not sure whether to laugh or cry.

"It aint fair, all you guys walking around here with all that good old testosterone shoved down the front of your pants and I can't have any."

"One day at a time, Abby."

"Yeah, well if we go out on call, we need to stop by a small home appliance store so I can pick something up."

The group from the Lieutenant's office had spotted Lavon and were waving trying to get him and Abby to join them.

Lt Crawford made the introductions "Deputy Police Commissioner Stewart, FBI Agent Tom Paterson, and Mayor's office Relations Sean Hardcastle, this is Detective Lavon Tyler and Detective Abby Blackwell, they are leading the investigation we have been discussing."

"Why don't I start by asking why you felt the need to sandbag us?" Agent Patterson asked.

"No one sandbagged you." The Lt answered.

"You are trying to get me to believe that you guys get a mob hit in an alley by two pros and trap them in a hotel in less than two days."

"It happens," Lavon answered.

Patterson stared at Lavon, not sure how the comment was intended.

"Look, there is no sandbagging, Tyler oversees the investigation, and he didn't even hit town until the night of the murders. And he has been giving regular daily reports to his boss" Stewart explained.

"You killed one of them, is that right?" Hardcastle confirmed.

"Yes, sir, that puts me on desk duty until the shoot is cleared."

"Can I tell the mayor it was you or him?"

"Tell the mayor the guy shot me before I shot him and if I wasn't wearing a vest it would be me in the box right beside that poor girl." Abby's tone was sharp.

"Do you guys have a plan going forward?" Stewart asked.

"Yes sir, since my partner is dry-docked, I am going to need help on the street with my next task."

"I can get you a detective, but they are in short supply, so it might be a while" Lt Crawford commented.

"On that note, you have Detective Howard out with broken ribs, concussion, contusion, and his jaw wired shut, what the hell happen to him?" Stewart asked.

"Train wreck," Abby answered.

"Boxing qualifiers, the men are aggressively looking to beat the firemen this year." Lt Crawford supplemented Abby's answer.

"Sounds like they are willing to die to do it," Stewart commented.

"If I could get Officer Bishop again. He worked with us in the alley the first night, and he helped spot the correct hotel the shooters were located in." Lavon tried to mop up the conversation.

"He sounds like to me he is involved already. And he has had eyes on our bad guy. By all means, let's get him, but are you sure he can handle detective work?" Stewart asked.

"Mostly, I need a street guide through the lower eighteen. I guess a uniform would know the area and the people better than anyone."

"Sounds like you already have a plan. Just no more sandbagging. Remember not everything is a jump ball" Patterson offered as a last word.

Chapter 14

"Who is it?" Big Foot asked. He had been lying on the bed, waiting for someone to get him out of Shepherds Pass. He had been all over the world and now he was stuck in a one-horse town that thought was the big city. His partner, Ramiro, had been shot by the lady cop. And where did that guy that chased him come from? The guy was fast and would have caught him if Big Foot had not thought to shoot the lady cop, getting out of the car. Still, most cops would have jumped over her and kept coming.

"Shelly, I got a message for you." A short girl that looked more like a schoolgirl than a hooker whispered into the door as Big Foot opened the door, with the chain still attached.

"God, you're big. I never did it with a guy quite as big as you."

"Look I don't know you."

"I was paid and told to keep you happy while the arrangement is being made." She lowered her voice and looked around to be sure no one could hear her. "Do you prefer boys? I could get you, someone."

Big Foot closed the door, removed the chain, and pulled her in. Shelly wore a loose print dress that was almost see-through. Big Foot pulled her close by grabbing the front of her dress so tight that it rose in the front to her thighs. With his other hand, he grabbed her reaching around and grabbing her butt firmly. "This is what I like."

Big Foot walked over to the bed and unbuttoned his shirt. "Perfect," Shelly said just before reaching her hand into her purse removing a silenced .9mm and firing two shots into the center of his chest. Big Foot hit the floor like a stone. Shelly walked slowly over and fired a parting shot into the center of his forehead. She removed a cloth from her purse and began wiping anything she may have touched.

WENDELL AND LAVON SAT down on the bench with Sugar in the middle. Sugar was a young white girl with a variety of tattoos. She had skinny legs and wore a plaid schoolgirl outfit. Sugar was covered in more makeup than any girl in her early twenties should ever need. In many ways, this girl reminded Lavon of Anita, one of his younger sisters. "I'm just sitting here Bishop; you didn't catch me with a John or any dope" Sugar offered as the pair sat beside her.

"I didn't come to bust you. I hear the next bust you could end up in Chillicothe."

"Please don't let them send me back there, I got my ass kicked twice a day and three times on Sunday."

"I just want to introduce you to a friend of mine. This is Detective Tyler."

"Hi, Sugar."

"Whatever your game is I don't want any part."

"It's not a game I have a picture here and I want you to see it." Lavon held the picture face down.

"No way I don't snitch."

"Fair enough. And I don't want you to tell me anything."

"Really. Then why do you want me to see the picture?"

"Because I am working homicide and the man in this picture is connected to seven local murders and the week is only half over." Sugar's eyes went wide.

"When he was trapped, he shot his way out."

"Then I don't want anything to do with that picture."

"See Sugar, Bishop told me he thinks you are a nice person at heart. That you may have had some bad breaks, but you never rip Johns off. And you don't spread rumors or lies." Sugar's face took on a half-smile as she looked at Wendell Bishop. Bishop was dressed casually because he had been instructed not to suit up. He would work for Lt Crawford as needed.

"Thanks, Bishop, I think you are nice too. Kind of bad the nice guys like square girls."

"Sugar, that's why I want to show you this picture. You don't have to tell me or anybody anything. But if you see this guy, make an excuse not to go with him anywhere. He shot two cops, and the cops are going to go gun happy when they see him. Bishop just doesn't want you hurt." Lavon turned over the picture. The was recognition on her face. Lavon started to stand up to walk away.

"He is in The Grand Motel room 214. But promise you will take care of each other and don't tell anybody I told you where to find him."

THE GRAND MOTEL LOOKED like it was a cookie-cutter version of the Deluxe where Lavon was staying. The only difference was it was more run down. People were congregating in the front of the structure, including a group of ragged old men passing a paper sack around. The building design was the horseshoe two level. It was still early evening by the time Lavon could get an entry team together, but the place was a beehive of activity. With the design, they could not enter the courtyard parking lot area until everyone was assembled, or they would have been announced prematurely.

"Alright, the manager unlocks the door, then dashes out of the way. The entry team hits the door hard. At the same time, the uniforms rush the ground, making sure no one can walk out into stray gunfire if there is any" The commander of the entry team yelled to his team

"Commander the ops a go, repeat go, go, go." Commanded the Lt from a safe position.

The entry team rushed to the door. The commander stepped out to the second-floor railing and called out.

"You may want to get the lead detective up here and somebody call the coroner."

"IS THIS A BAD TIME?" Lynn asked when Lavon answered his phone. He stood standing at the crime scene over the dead body of Big Foot. The news trucks arrived, and they were shooting footage everywhere.

"No, honey, it couldn't be better."

"I have a favor to ask."

"Sure."

"But you don't know what it is yet?"

"Does it involve dead bodies?"

"No, don't be silly?"

"Then sure. Whatever it is."

"Good, I already told my uncle you would be there. I need a dinner date for this evening and the truth is I was hoping we could duck out early and finish where we left off last night."

"What time?"

"Come to the house at seven." Lavon knew the medical examiner was ready to talk to him.

"See you soon." He hung up.

Chapter 15

Lavon was sure he was hallucinating when he entered the mansion with Lynn Masterson on his arm. Directly in front of him was Sean Hardcastle, the Relations man from the mayor's office he had met only that morning. Lavon then wondered if there was such a thing as a double hallucination because the person approaching from the right was Amber Dobb from Middle West Investments. "Well. Detective Tyler had I known you were up for grabs I would have tried harder" Amber and Lynn exchanged snotty glances and there it was. One of the things he was missing, the women looked alike and smelled alike.

A door opened and Lynn said. "Lavon, may I introduce my uncle, the honorable, Mayor Carlton J. Dodd" Lynn announced as she came out of her snit.

The air seemed thick with impending questions as the group sat down at the lavish dinner table. Lavon was hoping some of his questions would be answered without him asking.

"Sweetheart, how exactly do you know my cousin, Amber?" Lynn could not wait.

"Detective Tyler did me a big favor." Amber smiled a coquette smile.

"I want the juicy details." Hardcastle requested.

"He made arrangements for the investors' money to be returned after that blood bath."

"That sounds noble on the surface," Hardcastle noted. The mayor sat there carving away his food as if he expected nightly entertainment between his house guests and they were warming up.

"But didn't you tell me in a meeting this morning that you just got in town a few days ago?"

"That would be correct" Lavon confirmed.

"Then, by rights, shouldn't Detective Howard have the case you are working on?" All eyes stopped eating to see where the conversation was going.

"No, Abby Blackwell caught the case and I work with her."

"Thank you for clearing that up detective, because I heard a rumor that you beat up poor Howard so bad, he is eating through a tube."

Lavon sat back in his chair and put his fork down. There was a concerned look on Lynn's face, and it touched his heart that in such a short time, how she perceived him was so important to him.

"I don't know how people address each other here in Shepherds Pass but my father taught me that a man never draws a line in the sand and dares another man to cross it unless he is willing to protect his side of the sand."

The mayor clapped. "Was your father by chance a gangster."

"Worse sir he was police chief." This got a big round of laughs from everyone at the table. Lynn seemed pleased that Lavon had successfully defended himself from intellectual bullying as well as physical bullying.

"YOU HANDLED YOURSELF better than I would have expected tonight." Lynn proclaimed, lying naked with her head on Lavon's chest after lovemaking. They were at his place in the Deluxe Motel. His bed was much smaller, and the room looked overly basic.

"Now I know why you could not sign those papers the other day. The minute you saw your cousin's name you thought I was the biggest jerk on earth."

Lynn giggled a giggle both of confirmation and of relief that she was forgiven.

"I must leave town for a couple of days. There is a charity event back home and I have to be there. It was arranged before I got here." Lynn looked sad and the words of Nya came back. "Unless you want to go with me. You would meet my family, but I don't think my father owns an ascot." She began pretending to hit him.

"If that is a real offer, I'm all in. Let me clear my calendar. By the way, you seem like a sensitive guy to go around beating people up."

"Christian isn't synonymous with cowardice. History is full of stories where Christians have had to stand up and hold their ground, my lady." With that, he was asleep, while she stayed awake thinking of how to move him out of this dump.

Chapter 16

The following day was Thursday and Lavon had quite a few loose ends to clean up to be ready to leave town for the weekend. He brought donuts to Aaron, the lab techs, and thanked them for any added work he had caused. Lavon knew Abby, being one step from delirium tremors was in no shape to witness the autopsy of Big Foot. He also had a desire he was not sure about, and it was to visit Nya. But he knew he would see her with Wendell that night at Patrick's. Lavon was sure most of the work had been covered for his weekend off. When he looked up from his desk and saw Lt Crawford standing there waiting for a moment of pause. "I have here the official report of the money that was recovered in the alley. It has her lawyer's concoction. It was signed by Judge Waters and is now a matter of record." Lavon sat waiting for the portion of the conversation that would alter what had been said. "Ms. Amber Dodd is in my office and would like to speak to you privately." Abby rolled her chair close to hear the details of the lieutenant's conversation making sure there was no hint that she was eavesdropping. She wanted in on the conversation. "She seems to feel you may have a question or two that is off the record. She says you and you, alone and no recording devices."

"How do you feel about that Boss?"

"If she is a suspect do not stick your dick in her. If she has something to say, we need to know what it is before you take off. Remember, she is one of the mayor's relatives."

"With all due respect Boss, I know no one is asking me, but the other day Lavon deliberately slow-played her to gain her confidence and allow her to think her flirting was getting her somewhere. Now she shows up with the information he was trying to get. Please let him do his work." Abby's interjection seemed to stun Lt Crawford.

"So, you are saying it's part of the plan and you are not bothered that you are excluded from the interview?" The Lt confirmed.

"No ma'am. Let them use your office, and they will be always in view, and he can fill me in on what I need to know. In the meantime, she gets to run her seduction routine and he listens for clues to what is going on."

Lt Crawford led Lavon to her office and before leaving she whispered in his ear. "I don't know what you have been doing with Abby but keep it up. For a moment there, she sounded like the old Abby Blackwell."

Lavon smiled without comment.

"I AM HERE MOSTLY BECAUSE of Lynn. We were very close at one point. When I saw her at dinner, she was like a teenage girl falling in love for the first time with the handsome captain of the football team." Amber sat with her legs crossed in a visitor's chair. The small office surrounded by windows into the squad room did little to detract from her air of femininity. The room was covered with record boxes. Lavon took a seat facing her, consistently ignoring that curious eyes would be watching his every move. Amber's short shirt and low-cut blouse had channeled his attention and, fighting distraction almost impossible.

"The report doesn't say what the money was for" Lavon tried to redirect the meeting.

"Greenmail. As you guessed. The way it works is that there is a major construction project that is in the works. An amusement park is going to be built near here. It is a secret because if anyone found out they could buy a keystone piece of property and blackmail us into any price they want simply by holding up construction."

Lavon sank into his chair. "Secret does not always equal illegal. I get it. So why so much."

"The family that has the adjoining property is discussing opening a bunch of strip clubs, titty bars, and a casino and god know what else."

Lavon smiled. "That would be like Las Vegas opening next door to Disneyland."

"Now you see my problem.'

"What is the name of the family that is planning to open the clubs."
"Dodd."

"Say again?" Lavon was confused.

"That's right you are not from around here. The Dodds are two separate families from two brothers. The brothers left a legacy of cash and feuding."

"Which side is the mayor from?"

"My uncle and I are from the same side. Lynn however is not."

It was as if someone had grabbed him, and he sank in the chair now as if he wanted to descend through the back.

"Look, Lavon, take that look off your face. She is neutral in this mess. She was away at school when things got bad, the last time. She tries hard to be friends with both groups."

"Is she in danger?"

"Honestly, I don't know."

"Are you in danger?"

"At this point, I am hoping they got the message and will stop the old-school hit crap."

"SO, YOU ARE JUST GOING to abandon me for the weekend?" Abby asked.

"Every year the League of Christian Families holds an event in Lamont, Mississippi. Different families compete against each other for donations. The donations go to charity. The local elementary school is going to be able to upgrade the computer equipment they desperately need. So, yes, I am just going to abandon you."

"I feel an endless AA meeting marathon coming on."

"Remember, it has got to be for yourself, or it won't work. I have got a few things I need you to check out while I am gone, and I will call once a day to see where we are.

The shooting review board should have you released soon but if you need help contact Bishop."

"I don't want to sound sappy but thank you and thank you for not telling anybody."

Chapter 17

The drive from Shepherds Pass to Lamont, Mississippi, is about eight hours. The drive tends to be boring because there is little worth seeing. Seemingly endless stretches of smooth highway. Fields covered both sides of the roadway and in May everything was green. Lynn had fought falling asleep as she sat beside Lavon but at some point, the call of somnambule could not be heeded. Lavon drove his ragged old truck, praying to himself. God, please don't let her be a part of this mess and protect and keep her safe.

Lynn was startled awake by the hard-to-pin-down racket. She opened her eyes, and she and Lavon were parked in front of a large house. There were cars and trucks everywhere. The dozens of people milling about were socializing. There were groups of small children running and playing. One small child had a bubble pipe and bubbles flowed everywhere. "Is this the church group?" Lynn asked.

"No honey this is my family."

"Oh, God."

A stocky woman, with her hair flying in no set hairdo, ran to the pickup. "Lavon, I thought you would have been here earlier. Norbert and I have been here trying to keep a lid on everything. And not everybody is here yet" the woman scolded.

"How could that be?" Lynn questioned, surveying the mob.

"Alice, this is Lynn." Lavon introduced, but before he could complete the introduction Alice had opened to door and was pulling

Lynn out of the truck. Alice stopped and stepped back looking at how Lynn was dressed. "Are you a Mormon?"

"No."

"Well, it's alright to be a Mormon."

A man, closely resembling Lavon walked up, carrying a beer in one hand. "Damn boy, she is good-looking."

"This is my husband, Norbert. He is Lavon's older brother and a jerk in general. He doesn't know it is not polite to ogle your kid brother's woman. How would he like it if Lavon was checking me out" Alice offered?

A group of people poured toward them. One was a girl with a cast on her leg. The girl with the cast hobbled to Lynn and grabbed her around the waist. "I am so glad you made it" Lynn looked down confused in general but wonder who the girl was or why she was so glad to see her."

"It is polite to say your name before accosting a guest" Alice scolded.

"I'm sorry, I am Kimberly, Lavon's sister. When Lavon said he was bringing you, you got slotted for everything I can't do because of the cast. Now the Tyler girls don't have to forfeit anything."

"Any sign of Jody?" Lavon asked the surrounding crowd in general.

"Not yet" someone answered back. "Hey."

A young woman with a child on her hip called from the front porch. "The great man wants to talk to Lynn." Lynn wasn't sure she was ready to be separated from Lavon, but in the natural pushiness of Alice, she was grabbed and led to the house.

A short muscular man stood by the window of an apparent home office looking at the activities in the yard. There was a book on the desk with the back of the book facing up to reveal the picture of the authors. When the man turned around, it was him. He was the picture in the book. Sam Tyler had a grey buzz cut and a stern face but friendly eyes.

Lynn walked into the room and picked up the book. "Your son said you were a police chief."

"Retired my dear, I wrote for a couple of years as a ghostwriter, now they put me on the jacket."

"I have read a couple of your books. I had no idea."

"Judge Lynn Masterson."

"Yes."

"No."

"No?"

"No, these are family games, and every family is identified by the family name. I hereby, by the powers invested in me cancel your last name and dub you Lynn Tyler."

"Lynn Tyler?"

"I will try to remember to give you back your last name after the weekend is over. If you still want it back by then."

"This is all overwhelming."

"Agreed. Now the second part of our father-daughter talk. This is also the weekend of the Tyler prank and practical joke extravaganza. So, you know these idiots will be finding various ways to prank each other. Good luck"

"Good Luck?"

"Are you a Mormon?"

"No."

Sam Tyler walked to the door and opened it and screamed for Alice. Alice appeared instantly as if she had been waiting nearby.

"Find Lynn Tyler something that makes her look like a Tyler girl. For God's sake, she looks like a freaking Mormon."

Lynn looked for Lavon, but he was nowhere to be found. Lynn saw the woman that had been holding the small child seated on the couch changing an infant. Lynn sat down next to her, and a little blonde-haired girl started playing peek-a-boo with Lynn from behind a chair. When Lynn was not looking the little girl stumbled over to her and was holding up her arms to be picked up. Lynn could not resist. "The kids love this time of year because they don't have to fight over attention. There is always someone who wants to play with them. I'm Shelby, Lavon's sister."

"Nice to meet you."

"Did Noreen find you?"

"Who's Noreen?"

"She's one of my sisters and she is in Law school. She can't believe a real live judge is going to get involved in the nonsense."

Lynn had a question, but it was lost when she sighted a woman walking toward where she sat.

The woman was wearing sunglasses and a windbreaker. "Are you the one that is fornicating with my brother, Lavon?" The woman asked and everyone seemed to silence, waiting for the altercation to proceed. "Well, yes" Lynn answered. The woman unzipped her windbreaker and removed it. She had huge biceps and a strong body. More impressive, however, was the bone grip .9 mm that was in her waistband. "Then I just got one question for you missy. Are your intentions honorable or dishonorable?" She stood with her hand akimbo.

"So far, it has been pretty dishonorable," Lynn answered.

The women in the room all surveyed each other's faces. "Details, we want details." the muscular woman stated and brought all the women in the room to a roaring laugh.

"This nit whit is Sister Jody she is a state cop. What she failed to realize is that momma is due to be home anytime now and if she sees that gun in here with all these kids, she is going to paddle Jody's butt big time" Shelby told Lynn. Lynn felt she had survived her first Tyler practical joke, barely.

A SHORT TIME LATER a woman walked into the room she needed no introduction. Everyone treated her as their mother. "Ladies, it has come to my attention there is a new Tyler girl onboard" Rebecca Tyler, Lavon's mother announced. "It furthermore has come to my attention that she is not aware of our war cry." She looked at Jody who had returned without the gun. Jody yelled.

"Tyler Women take care of Tyler Men." there was a halfhearted response from some of the women. "Now that was sad. It was sadder than sad. That was pitiful." Jody walked to the center on the room. "Now, this time, on the count of three, give me all you got." Jody counted and the crowd was louder. "Again." They screamed the chant. "Like your life depends on it" Lynn found herself screaming right along.

The meal was excellent. Many of the women had worked together and the men did much of the cleaning, including dishwashing. There were enough people that no one person was overwhelmed, and everyone seemed to be having the time of their lives. That night, at the small motel where Lavon and Lynn were staying, Lynn sat watching Lavon, speechless. She now knew how he viewed life.

"Are you upset that we came?" Lavon asked, not able to read her mood.

"No, it's the most fun, so far, that I have ever had."

"You look a little down."

"Please don't think I am stupid or putting stuff in your head, but I wanted to take the baby home."

"The weekend is about family. It makes you examine the choices and the path you are on."

Lynn got into bed and wrapped herself in the blanket and huddled close to Lavon wrapping herself in his love.

Chapter 18

The first day of activities rocketed off to a quick start with a disembodied voice on an intercom requesting Lavon Tyler to report to the volleyball court. The men of the Tyler family had been challenged by the men of the other families. The Tyler men got to the court, and all took off their shirts and the women in the crowd went wild. All the Tyler men seemed to have a following of interested women that seem to overlap in the ages of the female fans. The men they were matched against seemed so jealous that they never seemed to recover. Lynn was amazed, not only at how athletic Lavon and his brothers were but how well coordinated their assault was on the competitors. There were enough Tyler men to rotate players and now they all had a chance to shine. The Tyler men took out the men they were opposing, took a ten-minute break, and then squashed another team as easily. Lynn jumped down from the bench in the stands where she sat, charged Lavon, and kissed him wildly. She caught herself just long enough to notice that the rest of the Tyler men seemed to be enjoying a similar reception.

"Judge Lynn Tyler report to booth 18." The disembodied speaker's voice commanded. Lynn went to booth 18, wondering why she had been referred to as Judge Lynn Tyler until she saw it was a pie-eating contest. Those idiots, she thought. At a table sat three people. One was a Bearded Man who weighed four hundred pounds easily. The next looked like a three-hundred-pound replica. The third was an obese woman covered in so much loose fat, it was hard to make out any shape at all, she appeared to be some form of oblong in a dress that looked like overstocked drapes. The timekeeper was a short man in a rumbled suit who could have weight not more than 90 lbs. He was shaky and resembled Don Knotts. The timekeeper started the contest and the 400 lb. guy won hands down. Now it was Lynn's job to present the ribbon. Lynn walked over to the big guy, and he scooped her up and kissed her holding her, lifting her from the floor. He released her and she barely caught her balance. She noticed the local paper was taking pictures of the presentations. When Lynn looked back at the crowd Lavon and Norbert were laughing so hard, they were falling on the ground. Lynn grabbed a cane from an old man and started beating both. "You jack assess set me up" she kept saying. "Lynn Tyler to the soccer field." the speaker's voice commanded, "Now what?"

"I have never played soccer before, and I am not going to start now" Lynn announced as she approached the group of Tyler women on the field. "No one is playing soccer, Lynn Tyler," Jody stated. "It's a tug of war and the count is not by weight but by the number of legs."

"We are short on legs, I thought you were going to replace me," Kimberly said in a sad voice.

"Okay, I got you, just give me the short version of what I have to do."

"You hold the rope, don't let go and you dig in. If our flag crosses the line, they win and, if we pull their flag over, we win" Jody explained. Lynn had still been confused by the pie-eating contest judge gag and the misunderstanding about the soccer field, she had not noticed there were 10 heavy-set women across a mud puddle from them. "Dig in with your legs, let those beasts wear down, then we yank the flag over" Jody called the strategy. The reality did not come anywhere near matching Jody's plan. When the whistle blew to start the game, the big women yanked and pulled all the Tyler women into the mud puddle one by one. The Tyler men stood shaking their heads as if disappointed by the defeat.

THE WOMEN NEEDED TO be hosed off before they were clean enough to ride back to the Tyler house. Lynn sat on the front porch, drying her hair with a towel and Rebecca Tyler came out of the house and sat beside her. Rebecca said nothing, she put her arm around Lynn and then rested her head on Lynn's shoulder. How could anyone transmit so much love and kindness without a single word? "Do the Tyler girls ever win the tug of war?" Lynn asked.

"No, we lose every year.

" Then why do you do it?" "Because you can't be a Tyler and only get involved in challenges where you know how it's going to work out. And you sure as hell can't only stand your ground only when you know you are going to win." It was a life lesson and now it rang home. Sometimes losing met learning. Lynn understood now all the families were there, not only to collect for charity but also to instill basic life values. Maybe some values her family had missed. "Come on into the house Lynn it's time to eat" Rebecca finally said in a mother's voice.

"Are you mad at me?" Lavon asked.

"No, actually I am kind of happy you felt good enough about things to include me. I did not, however, enjoy being molested by that mountain man."

"Well, it's hard finding victims for that, no woman comes back for seconds or forgets from year to year."

The two were lying in bed. Lavon had checked with Abby on her research and Lynn had checked in with her office.

"Your parents are great. I don't know how anyone could leave such wonderful people."

Chapter 19

On the second day of the event, Lynn had the chance to watch much of the interaction of many of the families. And she observed the people and saw it was all character-building. The competition was secondary at best. Lynn sat on a bench, watching two families compete in flag football and a girl sat down beside her, the girl was pretty but looked like she had some emotional issues. She wore a gray tee shirt that read Butler. Lynn looked over at the girl who was now staring at her, and a big fat girl sat on the other side of Lynn. The fat girl sat uncomfortably close.

"The program says you are Lynn Tyler. What's your real name?" The pretty girl asked, in a southern drawl, that was hard to discern.

"Why," Lynn asked.

"Cause you aren't no fucking, Tyler. You some home-wrecking piece of shit." The pretty girl's eyes were now on fire. Lynn could feel the hot breath of the fat girl on the back of her neck.

Lynn thought this must be a prank but, where is the off switch,

"Good to see you here, Casey" Lynn looked up and it was Jody standing there. Jody looked at the fat girl. "I'm going to beat the shit out of you and then stomp that tramp Casey in the ground."

"Look Jody maybe we made a misjudgment" the fat girl pleaded.

"Fair enough then, I am giving the two of you to the count of three to get off the grounds. One." Before two both women were running across the grounds. Jody sat down next to Lynn.

"What just happen, Jody?" Lynn asked.

"That was Lavon's old girlfriend, the one he caught fucking that guy." Lynn's heart started pounding. Jody did not know she did not know. "The thing is I introduced them "Jody kept looking toward the ground. "I feel like I fuck up my brother's life and there is nothing a sister can do to fix it." Lynn put her hand on the back of Jody's hand. "Lynn, I don't know if you and my brother are in love. I don't know if you are just screwing buddies or if you are his rebound girlfriend. But do me a favor. If you are his screwing buddy, be the best-damned screwing buddy a guy ever had. If you are his rebound girlfriend, be the best-damned rebound girlfriend a guy ever had cause no human being deserves to be fucked over like that."

THE TYLER WOMEN HAD a flag football game to play. The game had gone better than Lynn had expected, in that very little effort was required by her. Jody could bust down the field at a high pace. Sandra Max Tyer was a runner who ran marathons and triathlons. She did not even work up a sweat during the first half of the game. In the second half of the game the opposing team devised a plan to pull Sandra's flags the minute the ball was snapped, therefore putting her out of the play. They were afraid of Jody or would have done the same thing for her. The Davis's, the other team, had tied the score at 35 to 35, and it was the end of the fourth quarter. The Tyler woman had the ball on the midfield line. Anita Tyler called a huddle. " Alright, we are in a box we have to get the ball closer to be in range." "Can you throw for the end zone from here and we send Sandra the flash down to receive it? "Noreen asked. "Maybe, if I found a way to strap Jody's muscles on, I could throw the ball from here to Cleveland, but it would not be accurate, and a turnover means the end of the game we won't get it back."

"I have a play. We shift all except Lynn, to the strong side. You fake to me then pitch out to Lynn, and she runs for the sideline and gets enough distance to get you into range before stepping out." Jody suggested. There was something about the play that Lynn wanted to ask, but she just couldn't think of it.

Lynn had never been more scared in her life. Even meeting Casey had not frightened her nearly as badly as being part of the play. The ball was snapped, and everyone took off running their routes. The questions that had till now eluded Lynn popped into her mind. What if not everyone is drawn off their run by the fake, to the other side? Doesn't that mean she would be in the field unprotected? Surprising herself, Lynn caught the football. She took off running. The crowd sounded like the boom of a cannon, and she ran her fastest. Lynn looked over to her right there was a woman twice her size from the other team running after her. Lynn knew where needed to step out of bounds, but she was not there yet. Suddenly, over her left shoulder, she could see another Davis woman almost catching up with her. Lynn's heart pounded and her legs hurt but she kept running. How did athletes do this day in and day out, she asked herself. Crash! There was a great booming crash behind her. She looked over her shoulder and it was Jody, she had tacked one of the pursuing women, driving her into the other. The three ended up crashing into the local news booth. "Go for the lights of Broadway." Lynn heard Sandra yell, and Sandra showed up almost out of nowhere. She was ready to block for Lynn. Lynn crossed the goal line and tried to collapse, but the Tyler women lifted her on their shoulders and celebrated the victory as the time ran out.

One of the after-dinner traditions for the end of the weekend was karaoke. Before karaoke Sam offered his prayer and wished for the happiness of the family. Rebecca then stood up and spoke. "Tyler women, I took a head count and compared notes for grandchildren against some of the other grandmas out there and I found this crew is coming up short. So tonight, girls, when you go home." She paused and looked around the room "Put your backs into it." This brought a rousing cheer, followed by The Tyler men doing their karaoke version of Mick Jagger's "button your lip" with Sam Tyler doing his best Mick Jagger. The Tyler women followed with "Hearts for Sale" before the crowd dispersed.

"I AM MORE TIRED AND sore than I have ever been, but damn, I feel good," Lynn confessed back at the motel as she soaked in the tub. Lavon came into the bathroom and kneeled and began washing her back.

"Do we have to go back to the real world tomorrow?" Lynn asked but she noticed that Lavon was staring at her wedding rings again. She put her hand under the water.

"I met Casey today." The statement fell into the air and floated without substance and dissipated. "I am going to remove my rings for as long as we are together."

"Why."

"Because one of your sisters told me that the Tyler men are rough and tough, but there is one thing they cannot endure and that is infidelity. If my ring reminds you that I have ever been with another man, anywhere in my life, I should remove them or it's torturing you."

"Lynn, I cannot ask you to answer for anything you have done before we met."

"I love you, Lavon, and I don't want to be your rebound girlfriend."

Chapter 20

The only thing Jason Wellman hated about his job was working weekends while those above him never had to. Jason stood in his office at Middle West Investments collecting papers he would need to review before he could go to sleep that night, thinking about how much the world had changed over the last centuries. Here Jason had a degree in Law, one in business and another in Accounting and Finance and still through fate and events set into motion before his birth he served people far less intelligent than him. "Good night, Manny," Jason stated to the last security guard as he exited the building. And where is that tart Amber Dodd on a Sunday evening, probably somewhere getting her toes polished or her ass waxed or whatever rich white women do with their Sunday evening.

Jason saw a young woman on the ground on all fours like she had lost something. She was near his Mercedes. "OH." The young woman jumped as if startled as he walked up. "What are you doing?" "I dropped one of my contacts and I can't see well enough to find it," Jason smirked and started to walk closer to his car door. "Oh god no. If you step on it, I'll be blind for two days." Jason kneeled "Look sweetheart why do I help you look so I can get out of here." "Bless you." The woman kept feeling around on the ground. She had turned her back to where Jason was searching. Jason now noticed he was wearing a short skirt. He noticed the curve of her butt and the tone of her inner thigh. As she leaned forward in her search, he was praying for a slight glimpse of her panties. Just as she leaned forward, he saw she wore none. Jason sat up and loosened his tie to swallow and wiped the sweat from his face. It was hard to believe that the fat wrinkled creature he called his wife was the same species as what he had just witnessed. The woman turned toward him and reach into her purse and pulled out a silenced .9mm and before Jason could ever clear the thoughts of paradise from his mind she fired twice into his chest. She stood over him. His eyes were wide open looking at the shaved wonder before she fired the fatal shot into his head.

Chapter 21

"Gomer, you in there?" Abby yelled as she beat on the door of Lavon's Deluxe Motel room. She carried a large storage box. Lavon answered the door in his boxers. Abby pushed past him and let the box hit the floor. "Are you alone?" "Yes."

"Then do me a favor and put on some pants and a shirt or I swear to God I am going to rape you and you can arrest me after the afterglow." Abby made a couple of trips to the car bringing in boxes and coffee.

"Abby these are the original records you can't remove them from the building."

"I know that's why I told anyone asking I was moving them to the new building before I put them in my car."

"Don't you care you are breaking the law and anything we find may not be useable."

"Look sweet pants, you asked me to look up some stuff. The more I read the more I felt like a spy. I kept waiting for the bullet in the back of my head. Someone didn't want anyone to know a few things as I was hip deep in it and your butt was off on a hillbilly holiday."

Lavon looked at Abby staving off her anger and pointed at a box on the dining table in the room.

"What's that."

"It's a pie or two pies my mom sent them to you."

"What." She jumped up and rushed to the boxes.

"One is pecan and the other is apple she did not know which is your favorite."

"I need a fork." Abby started to search and found a fork and began eating. "God this is good; I want to marry your mother."

"Give me a minute while I decide if that is the most stupid or the most disgusting thing, I have ever heard someone say."

"Relay sonny Jim, I don't do girls, but I will tell you that with this sex fast even if I have never learned to play the piano, I have found new uses for my fingers."

"What is this?" Lavon was reading a report that was on top of the boxes.

With a mouth full of pie Abby answered. "Some of the Detectives have been turning in daily reports to join your butt kisser club. Nash and Coleman caught a homicide last night and they copied us on the daily because the guards told them we were there just the other day."

Lavon kept reading and Abby kept reading and eating.

"So, what did the princess tell you that she did not want me to hear?" Abby asked.

"That her family is two families in the middle of a fight over power."

"Well, everything here supports that. That is why I did not want to be going over this in the squad room. We are investigating not only the mayor's family but most likely the mayor himself."

After hours of reading and sorting Lavon and Abby made copies of some of the files and returned the original to the new building records room. They then headed back to the current squad room. A clerk ran up to them before they could reach their desks. "I got a bunch of messages for you two." Abby sat still guarding the box containing the remainder of the pies. She pulled out the fork and began eating again. The clerk was not sure if she had Abby's attention, so she addressed Lavon. "Patterson from the FBI would like a callback. Hardcastle from the mayor's office would like a callback. And some guy named Nolen Dodd says he is expecting you. Whatever that means" She sorted more messages. "For you separately Detective Tyler there had been a half dozen real-estate agents leaving messages for you to drive by and view some homes and give them a call."

The clerk looked at Abby still shoveling pie into her face. "Why is she eating like that." The clerk directly her inquiry as though Abby was no longer in the room. "Look no sex on booze on drugs and I have not been able to hold even water down in three days so if I want to eat a damn pie let me eat it." Abby's rant has caused a crowd of sympathetic coworkers to gather.

Chapter 22

Lavon took the opportunity to brush pie crumbs off Abby as they waited in the waiting room of Nolen Dodd. Unlike the mayor's office or his home, Nolen Dodd's office was in the lower eighteen. It was in the lower half of the eighteen blocks making it technically in a bad neighborhood, but it was the cleanest building on the block. From any angle, it looked like a small bank or credit union. People scurry about with little resemblance to their false images portrayed in cinema and books. "They will see you now?" The receptionist an elderly woman with bifocals on a chain announced leading them slowly into the office. Nolan Dodd was a powerful-looking man in a grey three-piece suit. He was in his early sixties but had a strong age-defining face and brown eyes that resembled the eyes Lavon noticed in Amber and Lynn. A woman in her sixties in a flowing dark blue dress sat on a sofa in the office watching them as they entered.

"You must be Detectives Tyler and Blackwell." He stood and offered his hand. "This is my sister Joanne she is involved in day-to-day operations and wanted to sit in on this meeting." Nolen smiled a fearless smile.

"You wanted to see us?" Abby asked.

"Yes. But first, let's clear the air. First, I don't take offense that you sat down to dinner with my cousin the panty waste mayor before coming to meet me even though you are sleeping with my niece."

Abby was frozen waiting for Lavon's denial.

"Sir, with all due respect I am from a family of fourteen children. There is a host of children and children of children. Then there are brothers-in-law and sisters-in-law and that is a hell of a lot to keep up with. I got here a week ago from Lamont Mississippi and even being able to keep up with my clan I am still am at lost as to understanding which Dodd is which."

JOANNE CHUCKLED AND Lavon was not sure if it was his accent or if she sympathized with his circumstances.

"Furthermore, sir I have never slept with a woman that I was not romantically attached to so for the sake of this conversation please, even if you don't want to show respect to me as a Detective show some respect to her and don't insult her dignity."

For a moment Nolen and Lavon stood staring at each other.

"He sounds like you Nolen, that's what she sees in him."

Nolen held out his hand to shake again. Lavon accepted and all sat.

"Can we talk about the murders?" Abby asked.

"I did not have anything to do with them, but I don't expect you to believe that. See the problem with being the bad guy is that when a good guy wants to get away with a crime, they frame the bad guy."

"Detectives, Morris Tanner and I were lovers for years. We never married because his children from his late wife never liked me." Joanne explained. "He died in that alley. If we set up the ambush, there is no way in hell we would not have sent someone else." Joanne had the look of a widow in mourning, and it was what made her statement make sense.

"What can you tell me about the Masterson's?" Lavon asked.

"The Masterson's worked for us during the old days. Donald Masterson was one of the best enforcers. Lynn married him thinking she had reformed him." Nolen paused to look at Lavon solely. Lavon knew that was why Nolen had been so hard on him. Nolen was protecting the part of Lynn he had fallen for. The part of Lynn that had not always chosen men wisely. Lavon also knew Abby was unaware of his thinking but an interview like this comes seldom and he had to take full advantage. "Was the money in the alley for you?"

"Yes, it was a legal transaction."

"Greenmail."

"Yeah, so it's legal."

"Who from the other Dodd family arrange the cash drop?"

"Amber." Joanne spit out as if she had great disdain for even having to use Amber's name.

"Since no one has said to let me be the first. You think someone from the other side of your family is trying to wipe you out by making you look like out-of-control, guns-blazing gangsters?" Abby concluded.

Lavon was happy that Abby had held it together and had not shown how little she knew before the meeting started.

"YOU GOD DAMN RED RECK meathead how could you let me lie to the Lieutenant like that?"

Amber had driven only a few blocks after the meeting and had pulled over to explode on Lavon.

"Abby."

"I'm Detective Blackwell to you, cocksucker."

"You did not lie to the Lieutenant. I haven't touched Amber. I am involved with Lynn, his other niece."

"Lynn, not Lynn as in Judge Lynn Masterson."

"That's the one"

Abby started laughing uncontrollably. "Maybe they should have given you a Shepherds Pass history lesson before letting you come here."

"At least you are getting your sense of humor back even if it is at my expense."

"Alright from now on if we work as partners, we are partners. Don't just tell me the stuff that you think I might need to know. Let me know what you know."

"Deal. When can I start back calling you Abby when no one is around."

They both stared at each other for a moment. "I just had a really bad thought about all of this," Abby stated. "So did I."

Chapter 23

"Excuse me young lady but what exactly is this?" The small Japanese woman seated her husband in the courtyard of the Chinese restaurant asked the waitress. The waitress was a young Chinese American girl in her twenties. Her hair was shaved into a spiky buzz cut with the top spray painted purple.

"That's the tea you ordered."

"That's not tea. Don't you have any real tea? What do you drink?"

"Beer mostly." The waitress smiled and turned to walk away but the woman stopped her. "Where are you from?" "Here." The Japanese husband seeing no joy in the exchange decided to help as best he could.

"I think my wife is asking where your parents are from."

"California."

"And your grandparents?"

"Not quite sure somewhere overseas. I think China." The waitress wandered off.

"Do you think we have time to stop back by here and kill her? We would be doing a public service?" The wife asked.

"We'll make the time."

THE YOUNG WOMAN DID not like having to catch the train but those were her instructions. She checked her bags but did not like being that far from her .9mm. She looked up and saw an older Japanese gentleman walking toward her trying to read something from a strip of paper. "Excuse me young lady I'm new here. What does this word say?" He asked in broken English. The young woman leaned forward to see the paper and it was the last thing she ever did. The Japanese wife shoved a spike through the rib intercostal spaces puncturing the lower ventricle of the heart allowing the blood to pump out to the open spaces of the young woman's chest. Even if a surgeon had been standing there, he would not have been able to save her. The Japanese couple sat the girl down gently in a seat. The woman closed her surprised eyes and the couple scurried off to exit at the next possible stop, for their return to Shepherds Pass to find the horrible waitress from this morning's breakfast.

"YOU KNOW. TERRELL, it used to amaze me back when I played football how guys as big as you could move so fast and be so quiet." Lavon's stood near one of the windows at the courthouse and a shadow overcame him. He knew it was Terrell. Lavon had no idea if Terrell would respond back or even if he had the ability. Finally, Terrell spoke. "She showed me a picture of her being hoisted by a group of women while raising a football. She says she scored the winning touchdown."

Lavon smiled remembering the pride on her face that day and the kid that wanted to talk to her.

"She is happy again after a long time. For years she was just a shell of a person."

"Were you around when she was married?"

Terrell grunted in the affirmative.

"Was he a bad guy?"

"Piece of shit. Womanizer. The type that rubs it in the wife's face."

"The report says he was shot by a bugler he was surprised." Lavon offered.

"No, it was murder. But no cop in North America was coming to the defense of a piece of shit like Donald Masterson. I think most cops think the judge ordered the hit."

"But not you?"

"No, I am like a babysitter to these judges. I know real sadness and remorse. I see hundreds of women come through here that have offed their husbands and cry lakes of fake tears. So, I know the real from the fake. She could not break free emotionally from him no matter how badly he treated her."

"Did you kill him?"

"No, he was shot. I would have used my bare hands."

A session broke out for the court and Lynn walked out.

"Were you waiting for me to ask me to dinner?"

"That and to tell you I love you." Lavon turned around and Terrell had disappeared.

"Wonder how they do that." Terrell was no longer standing there.

"Who. Do what?" Lynn asked.

"Never mind."

Chapter 24

"I have an idea. Since you don't have time to look at houses why don't I contact one of your sisters to come and help find a place."

Lavon and Lynn were having dinner at the outside tables at the Warf restaurant. Lavon sat staring at the waters of the man-made lake lost in thought. Lynn reached her hand across the table and touched his hand. Lavon looked down and noticed she had removed her wedding rings.

"You took them off."

"Cause I'm yours."

Lavon looked into her eyes.

There is something in the case you are working that is bothering you?"

"A little." He confessed.

"Lavon, there are going to be times when things in my work may make me a little distant for a short while. Do you plan on stopping loving me when that happens?"

Lavon shook his head.

Then whatever it is deal with it. But tonight, I got you and you have me, and I say we finish dinner and go to whichever bed is closest yours or mine and we make love like two people who love each other should. Tomorrow will take care of itself."

Lavon knew that she was releasing him of responsibility for anything he was wondering about. It was the push he needed to rise from his lethargy. They rushed to the Deluxe Motel on the other side of the bridge. Once in Lavon's room and made love and helped each other heal emotional scars caused by misplaced trust in past lovers. Some of the best love known to man or woman.

Chapter 25

"Get away from my desk Nash." Lavon walked up and could hear Abby arguing with someone.

"You must be Tyler. I saw you dismantle Howard in the ring." The Detective with Nash, Dee Coleman stated to Lavon as he walked up.

Dee squeezed Tyler's arm. "Hey, my now ex-boyfriend screwed my sister, are you free to go over and fuck him up," Coleman asked Lavon.

"That doesn't sound nice. What's up?" Lavon asked.

"We'll this is the team that caught the murder of the Lawyer over at Middle West. Now they say it's our case" Abby synopsized.

"The Lawyer Jason Wellman took two to the chest and one to the head." Nash began.

"So?" Lavon asked.

"So, he would have survived the chest wounds because he was wearing a better vest than we get issued. The tap to the head came back and it's the same gun that shot Big Foot." Nash explained.

"So, we check footage of security from the Middle West which was no easy task," Coleman stated before Lavon interrupted.

"Why not?" Because everyone there kept saying the tapes can only be released with the permission of the lead company lawyer."

"Let me take a wild guess. That would be the guy with a hole in his head." Lavon sat down knowing this was not going to go away soon.

"We finally got an Amber Dodd to release the tapes. We get a make on the girl shooter. Train stations show her board a train for Wichita.

We got the transit police to stop the train in Kansas City. And there she is."

"So, bring her back," Lavon asked.

"No, my southern friend we now get to the best part." Abby teased.

"They lost her," Nash stated.

"So, she is on the run in Kansas City. Would that be Missouri or Kansas."

"Doesn't make any difference country boy. When he says they lost her he means. She was dead on the train. Some form of Kakazu heart stab and now they don't know where the body is." Abby clears up.

"So, you guys are trying to hand us a homicide case with a missing body?" Lavon asked. "You do know if this was happening to anybody else it would be funny."

"It gets better," Abby stated.

Lavon's hands sank into his hands. "How could it." He mumbled.

"Transit realized they never removed the lady's luggage from the train, and it was picked up in Wichita. Wichita police found the gun and silencer in her luggage and ran the match through the database." Coleman explained.

"Set off alarms like the fire suppression system in hell." Abby joked.

"No doubt," Lavon muttered.

"The FBI wants to find out what type of shit show we are running," Nash stated.

"Lt is in a meeting all day with the building commission trying to get us out of this place a little quicker," Nash stated.

"It's in the Kansas City morgue," Lavon said.

"WHAT?" ABBY ASKED.

"Listen to what you guys are saying. The body showed up in one place, the hot weapon showed up in another state. Someone categorized the body as a gunshot, but you said she was stabbed."

"They have the body miss categorized."

"Have them look again and they will find it," Lavon concluded.

"Okay Solomon, who's case, is it?" Abby asked in a smart mouth tone.

"Solomon said split the baby. We work on it together until the Lt splits it up. God, know we got enough dead bodies and crime scenes to go around." Lavon stated.

"I like this guy. Are you dating anyone here yet? I mean hanging out the Abby you are probably hungry for a real woman." Coleman offered.

LAVON AND ABBY AND Nash and Coleman worked together to combine the evidence thus far collected. They had to duck calls from the FBI and the Mayor's public relations office.

Lavon was happy that the group could answer some of the questions he had about the relationship between Lynn and her late husband. He was glad to see that the previous investigation showed that she was in St. Louis at Washington University lecturing when the death occurred. This made him wonder if her being absent with such an easily verifiable motive was planned.

One clear thing is that there was at least one more assassin in town. But where and who was doing the hiring? But Lavon figured they were on to something. They now had an idea what was going on if not who was doing it. At some point, they may be able to channel the activities and then arrest the person involved.

Chapter 26

L avon walked to Patrick's over the bridge from his motel and saw Nya seated with a beer in front of her. He sat "Hi Nya."

"Hello Lavon, the beer is for you."

"Wendell was delayed with work."

"I guess you will just have to put up with my poor company for now."

"I wanted to talk to you alone anyway, Lavon." Nya looked serious and a little sad.

"What's wrong?"

"I made a mistake."

"So, let's fix it."

"The mistake is I did not know how much a friend you would become to Wendell."

"Why."

"Because all my life people have made a joke of my reading the future from their palm and it's just that a joke in most cases. You see I do see things, but I can tell people because they never believe it."

"I don't understand Nya."

"There was a grave experience in your palm. Possible death and loss of heart. But knowing this. Having this gift people confuse it with causation. Like I cause it or can change it. I cannot."

"Does it matter if I don't believe in it?" He smiled to ease her burden.

"IT IS NOT MY CALL TO challenge your belief system. And in no way do I wish to cause you pain. I only ask that you be careful the next few days."

"Nya, in the Drake when that girl was shot. She looked like you. Was she a relative?"

"No maybe a reflection."

Lavon noticed a man standing at the bar. There was something about the man that did not fit. The man was in his forties with a grey crew-cut hairdo like a marine. He had the body of a teenage athlete, and his sharp blue eyes were constantly surveying the room.

"Wendell told me to tell you that if you help him get his stripes we can marry and name our first child Lavon after you unless it's a boy."

Lavon kept watching the man.

"It has begun hasn't it." Nya's voice sounded far off to Lavon. His attention was redirecting. What was so wrong with this guy?

"If I see you again it will be in three days." Lavon thought he heard Nya say as he stood to walk over to the soldier at the bar.

"Excuse me sir but I am with the local police, and I was wondering if I could see some ID." Lavon requested.

"Sure thing." The soldier sat his beer down. The next thing Lavon knew he was flying backward over a table from the force of a spinning back kick. The man had taken off running toward the bridge.

"No. Not this time." Lavon uttered. And began pursuit. Lavon ran often and had run for years. He ran with one of his sisters who ran on a national title level so he knew this race was moving a hell of a lot faster than he would have expected. Lavon started pushing people out of the way yelling that he was the police. He was in the middle of the bridge before Lavon caught him and tackled the soldier. Both men sprang to their feet and the soldier shot a front snap kick, but this time Lavon was ready. The soldier closed the distance between them with a spinning backhand that Lavon blocked and hit the man in the ribs hard. Lavon noticed this man was more solid than anyone he had ever fought. The soldier countered and smacked Lavon with an elbow that landed in his face. Lavon shot a left jab followed by a right and the soldier looked into Lavon's eyes and smiled with a look that said at last a challenge. Lavon kept punching and landing many of the shots he knew this guy had too much training in foot fighting to step back from him. The soldier head-butted Lavon and Lavon fell to one knee. The soldier pulled out his gun at the same time as Lavon.

Both men grabbed the wrist of the other to keep aim impossible. The was a single loud explosion as both handguns went off at the same time. The men were so close together that the explosions went off under their arms near their ribcages. Both men were bleeding and burned from the close exploding of weapons going off.

"Stop. Police." Someone yelled from the north side of the bridge. The soldier let go of his grip, jumped back, and kicked Lavon. Lavon when down to one knee again and so did the soldier. Both guns had now fallen on the ground and the soldier's gun was closer. The soldier recovered his gun and then looked into Lavon's eyes. The soldier fired his gun over Lavon's head at the charging officers who now were ducking and jumping in the water to escape being shot. The soldier winked at Lavon and ran south on the bridge. Spectators had collected on the south end of the bridge taking pictures and video of the altercation. The soldier pointed his gun at the spectators and fired. They quickly got the message to clear him a path. The spectators started diving into the water. Lavon picked up his gun. He did not know how much pursuit he had left in him.

He was beaten, burned and bleeding but so was his prey.

"Drop the gun asshole." someone yelled from behind Lavon. Lavon turned and looked into the barrel of a gun being held by a rookie officer.

"I'm the cop you moron." The rookie smacked Lavon in the face with the gun rolled him over when he fell and was handcuffing him when the last thing Lavon heard before blacking out was Wendell's voice saying.

"You idiots mugged the Detective and let the suspect go."

Lavon had the notion of a small Indian woman sitting on his chest shoving a tube down his nose and lights all around him. His head was spinning, and his consensus drifted in and out. Lavon saw Lynn running for the goal line. Then he saw his mother sitting on the back porch in Lamont with a small boy sitting between the two of them. He looked closer and he was also the small boy.

"Somebody, get some of these fucking cops out of here."

He heard someone yelling.

"Does anybody know this guy's medical history?" A woman yelled through the haze.

Lavon felt he had been visited by Nya and he had confronted her and asked her if she had psychic abilities and if so, why had she not warned him. He remembered her telling him that the journey for Lamont to Shepherds Pass had taken him to a place where there was a difference in how many things functioned. He was now in a place where time and space held no lock on the strength of relationships and some of his close friends must be people, he was only recently meeting.

Lavon could hear Nya telling him his relationship with love was not bound, it was free to explore. He could not remember when she visited or how, even though he still had the tube in his throat they had spoken. But rest seemed more important than simple answers since his mind and body seemed in a race to heal and both seemed to be fighting for last place. Good, he thought at least I am still alive. Next time soldier to the death.

Chapter 27

"**A** t this time, we are asking everyone to clear the courtroom. Please exit in an orderly manner. You will receive notice as to the rescheduling of your court date. We appreciate your cooperation." Terrell announced before walking over to the bench. Judge Lynn Masterson was doing night court and she had a full house.

"What's going on Terrell, another fake bomb threat?" she asked humoredly.

"No ma'am. I just got word a cop is down in the field."

She looked at him waiting for him to say the words.

"It's Detective Tyler he is in bad shape."

"I've already made arrangements."

Before he could finish his statement, Lynn had catapulted from her chair and was out the courtroom door.

ABBY HAD JUST FINISHED an AA meeting and was sitting with her sponsor when she got a text. "Sorry, I got to go that moron needs me."

LAVON'S EYES OPENED. Or at least he thought they were open. He gazed out of the murky swamp that is haziness. Around him, the scale that measures reality seemed out of balance. Was he unconscious for moments or days? No way to know. Slowly he began waking and the dream state that comprised the very fabric of our dream started to fall to ash in the pile of nothingness where our subconscious debris lay dormant waiting for the next dream state to recover it. He saw a head on his chest and thought the thing he wanted most in the world at this time was to have Lynn there to confront him. For a moment he was afraid to reach out and touch the figure for fear that it might too be an illusion and turn to ash as he touched it. He slowly raised his right arm and touched her hair. Thank you, God she is real. She is here. I don't care if she is mad at me for anything I said or did wrong. Life will go on. I don't care if she was a part of the criminal threading that wove the fabric of this screwed-up town. My heart beats as her heart beats she is mine.

"Welcome back brave warrior," Lynn whispered.

"How long?" Lavon asked in a dry rasp. Lynn got him water to sip through a straw.

"Almost three days."

"Did anyone catch him?"

"No, but you are famous." She smiled. "Some people caught the fight on their cell phones, and you made social media big time. Especially, the part where your guys beat the shit out of you and were handcuffing you."

"I was hoping that part was a dream."

"No such luck. The mayor is pissed."

Lavon smiled.

"I have been in constant contact with your family.

The was some allergic reaction to something they gave you in the emergency room and it was lucky that I could get in touch with your mother to explain it to them."

"You saved my life."

"Don't be so grateful just yet. I check you out of that roach motel you were living in, and Jody came up to help me move you into my guest room."

Lavon rolled his eyes but decided to conserve words due to the strain on his throat.

"Your father told me to remind you that there is a reason cops have partners. And that they have a new thing called calling back up. You might want to try it next time you are fighting a robot on a bridge."

"Gee, that guy was good."

"Some ex-special forces fight instructor or something, Abby is supposed to fill you in when you get better."

"How soon can I blow this place?"

"That had better be a Tyler joke."

"He is still out there, Lynn."

"I saw the guns go off on the bridge. He is probably hurt as bad or worse than you. He is probably somewhere recovering waiting to get the hell out of town. I know I told you I would not interfere in your job, but baby please don't go head-to-head against that guy again."

"Can I ask you a question about your family?"

"Sure."

"When you were younger were you and Amber good friends?"

"Strangely enough we were the best of friends. Most people thought we were sisters because of the similar looks but also because she started dressing a lot like me."

"Did all that end about the time you married Masterson?"

"Shortly after as I recall. She started getting snippy. And acting jealous. Why?"

"Is there anything pink in the guest room?"

"Smart ass I will have the whole room painted pink while you are in here."

Chapter 28

Amber walked into Court 14 with her lawyer Bernard Epstein close by. Lavon had asked her to meet to clear up a few things not covered in the prepared statement.

When she walked into the room the first thing, she noticed was that Lynn Masterson was seated in the witness chair, with Lavon standing beside her. Amber looked over and saw at one of the tables that there was a woman with a technician preparing to take the meeting. In the spectator stands were Lt Crawford and Paterson of the FBI.

"Well, what all is this?" Amber questioned. Lamont rushed to her to draw her and her lawyer to the seats he wanted them to take.

"As you know we have a string of murders, and I was hoping we could clear a few things up.

So that no one is blindsided I thought as irregular as it is we could combine the interview and move on. Judge Masterson, being a lawyer, herself is her without consul." Epstein looked this great suspicion at Tyler. "Are you Mirandizing my client at this time?"

"No. That was not my plan, but if you feel that is necessary maybe we should."

"No. Not at this time."

"I tell you what, why don't we ask your client not to answer anything until directly asked? That way we can explain why the questions are based on what we have learned and if there is a contradiction the two of you can work on the correction. And we are recording for the record." Lavon smiled.

"Okay, but I don't like theater so if there are any proposed melodrama we are out of here."

"Yes, sir I wouldn't have it any other way." Lavon looked over at Lt Crawford and winked.

She nodded in return.

"Wendell, could you bring our other guest in."

Lavon called and Wendell walked in with Mayor Carlton Dodd. The mayor looked agitated but said nothing. He sat where requested and Wendell looked relieved to have the man out of his sole care.

Wendell walked over to Lavon and handed him a cell phone. Lavon set the phone on the defense table in front of him.

"Will this take long; I am a busy man?" The mayor finally revealed a restrained burst of impatience.

"Well, I hope not because I have something I need to do shortly," Lavon answered then turned toward the outer entry doors. "Abby, could you show our other guest in?" Abby walked in the Nolen Dodd and his sister Joanne. The mayor stood and stared at Nolen with anger. "If I had known this clown was going to be here, I would not have come," Nolen stated as Joanne just sneered.

"Yes, sir, and believe me you are free to leave at any time. But a few things I will cover in the questions and how I came to my conclusion, right wrong or indifferent need to be said in front of both sides of the family at the same time. That way I show no favor."

A far greater note of seriousness overtook the room. "So, ask my client your questions, this room is getting a little stuffy," Epstein commanded.

"Yes, sir some basics first. Lavon explained that the woman in the room with the tech was from the District Attorney's office and she was taping all the interviews regarding the case. Lavon stated that since the case might be handed over to the FBI Patterson had agreed to sit in.

He then when through introductions for the benefit of the record and a statement regarding their voluntary participation.

Lavon walked over to Lynn and placed his hand on the banister in front of her. "I would like to start with a statement from you Judge Masterson. Lynn's eyes opened wide revealing she had no idea what he was up to.

"Am I correct that you were married to the late Donald Masterson?"

"Yes, everyone here knows that."

Lavon thought she seemed a little shaky. They thought it might be because she could see he was still injured.

"Judge Masterson, do you remember someone yelling to you recently to turn on the lights of Broadway?"

A look of puzzlement swept the room, except for Lynn who smiled. "I sure as hell do?"

"What did it mean?"

"It meant you have a clear path to the end zone. So, I ran for the winning touchdown."

Lynn seemed so proud of herself.

"It was a women's flag game for charity."

There was murmuring among the crowd.

"This is turn on the lights of Broadway time again, are you ready."

"Yes, detective ask your questions."

"What type of man was Masterson?"

"He was a hard man. Tough. The ultimate bad boy."

"And you married him."

"I thought at the time to truly become a woman you had to tame a tiger. I was wrong."

"Excuse me detective what does this have to do with my client?" Epstein asked.

"We're almost there, sir."

"Judge I know it's painful but was Masterson unfaithful."

Lynn looked like she had run out of tears for Masterson. "Totally."

"During some of my questioning with someone we both know, they told me that Donald Masterson used to like to throw his affairs in your face when it served him. Is that true?"

"Yes, that was the way he played it."

"Do you remember telling me that you and Amber were so close that people thought you were sisters?"

"Why, yes."

"When I first thought about it, I thought maybe you copied her. But that is not the truth she copied you, didn't she?"

"Why yes. Is that a problem?"

"The problem was her perfume. It is custom-made to copy yours."

"I never noticed."

"She copied you right up until marriage until you now had the one thing she could not replicate."

Lynn stopped looking at Lavon and stared at Amber. "You deranged bitch you were fucking my husband."

Amber smiled. "That shit is ancient history."

"Not so ancient Amber, see when I looked at the file it would appear several detectives dropped the case and sent it to cold cases. I think they thought the judge did it and felt like she deserved to go free.

But if they had known he had an angry mistress you would have been under a microscope."

Amber started to retort but the lawyer grabbed her arm.

That right Mr. Epstein restrain her because I haven't asked the question yet. Because we all know how it went with Donald. He fucked her then when she told him she wanted him to leave Lynn for her.

He laughed in her face. He was going to tell Lynn anyway. To him, you were just another cheap piece of ass."

"You should have seen the so-called bad boy beg for his life before I pulled the trigger," Amber screamed before even she knew what came out of her mouth. Lavon looked down at the cell phone, then over to Wendell who threw up both hands in a curious motion.

"Well since we are still on schedule let's talk about a different matter if counsel will permit. I promise since we need to deal with the murder of Masterson separately, I won't bring him up again. But we do need to ask about the other murders. The six in the alley and Jason Williams."

Epstein sat there looking defeated wondering what to do next. Lavon hobbled toward the place where Amber sat and spoke. "You know I have an Uncle Oscar who is a salesman and he told me something that came to me while I was unconscious."

"What that you are a hillbilly pea picker, and you always will be." Amber sneered.

"That's a given but what he told me otherwise was a good salesman has a pitch that works. The reason it works is practice. Practice. Practice. But the problem then becomes that you repeat it so much you don't even hear yourself talking."

Amber slid into her chair as if she was bored.

"When I guessed the money in the alley the day of the murders was greenmail and you confirmed that."

"So," Amber said, and the lawyer grabbed her arm, and she pulled it away in defiance.

"So that means I know what greenmail is."

"I still don't get it."

"Then let me break it down. When I pulled up in this town my first thought was that I had landed in another universe." Most of the room chucked. "You see greenmail is usually legal and usually done in a bank or an investment office.

You have perfectly good building then why did you send those men to that alley." Amber said nothing and Lavon looked at her lawyer. "Don't worry I know the answer. You sent those men to slaughter."

Lavon then looked at Joanne. "God ma'am I am so sorry, but we must clear this up too."

"Fire this son of a bitch." Amber screamed. "You are the goddamn mayor." She looked at Mayor Dodd. Mayor Dodd looked back in disappointment. Amber looked over at Nolen. Lavon smiled and winked at Joanne. "What was that for?" Amber asked, having caught the wink.

"It's called a tell my whore friend. It is where a gambler accidentally reveals the strength or weakness of his hand." Joanne stated, with a cruel look in her eye.

"Now I don't get it?" Epstein who now looked like a man whose clothes had been washed with him still in them questions.

"Simple she made the same sale pitch to both sides of the Dodd family, the ones trying to build the casino and the ones trying to build the amusement part. Remember when I said salesmen somethings don't listen to their own sales pitches?

Well, when you visited my office, you explained what a keystone is. If I told you, it was greenmail that would mean I know what a keystone is. First, I just thought it was my country accent. Some people think anyone with an accent sounds dumb and therefore must be dumb. So, I checked the Keystone, the piece that would hold up development if in the lower eighteens and you owe it. You are the one holding up the development while you pillage both sides of your own family."

A murderous look shot through the room. Amber now had a kid caught with his hand in the cookie jar look. The cell phone rang. It was Sugar, the prostitute that Lavon had recently met. Lavon motioned to Wendell and whispered something in his ear then Wendall ran from the room on an apparent arrand.

"Detective given what has been discussed I have to know on what charges are you going to hold my client?" Epstein asked.

Lavon had the look of deliberation on his face but knew what was next. "That is up to your client. She needs to pick an option. Option

A we arrest her for the murder of Donald Masterson and all the recent murders related to the swindle she has been running. This offer is only available with a confession which the District Attorney's office is willing to take right now. Option B is she does not confess in that case Mr. Patterson and the FBI take her into custody and arrest her for RICO violations and they freeze all her assets. You may need to switch to a public defender because they will freeze assets back to the first milk money you got in kindergarten if they can. Not a good choice because I will tell you she will be required to name names and that could be a death sentence."

Both Nolen and the mayor looked at their niece in total disgust.

"And of course, there is option C. We don't arrest and let her take her chances on the streets with both sides of the Dodds knowing she played them."

Wendell rushed back into the room waving a piece of paper. "I hate to put a time crunch on this, but you have two minutes to decide. I have a raid to get to. It took less than the two minutes Epstein yelled.

"She will take option A." Lavon handcuffed Amber allowing her to start her statement with the District Attorney.

Lynn motioned Lavon over to where she sat the grabbed him by the collar. No fighting, do you hear me? Abby walked up and slammed a vest into Lavon's arms. "Put that on." Then turned to Lynn. "Don't worry I'll take care of this jackass."

"Hey Patterson, we are going to pick up that special force's robot guy, want to come alone? We have an entry team waiting on the perimeter."

Chapter 29

It was a different room in the same Grand Motel that the police entry team now crash open the door. They found the soldier. He was barely conscious. He had been paying prostitutes to bring him medical supplies while waiting for contact with Amber, which never came.

"So why didn't you shoot me on the bridge?"

Lavon asked the half-conscious wreck that they pulled out on the gurney.

"You know why. That was the best fight I have had in years. Guys like you and me live for the last fight and we want it great.

Those pussies were coming to break it up."

"Let me tell you a secret. You are a lot better than me." Lavon revealed.

"Then get ready. Next time we meet on a bridge, and no one stops us till one of us is dead, No tear or remorse."

"HEY, YOU GUYS GET THE girl why don't you give us the soldier? The best you get him for is the attempted murder of a cop. I think he is linked to a string of pro-jobs." Patterson asked.

"Clear it with the Lt and he is all yours."

Lavon asked.

"Do you think he killed the little hit girl and put her on the train?"

"Nope. Not his style. Besides.

Have you ever been on a marine base?"

"No, why?"

"Because everybody looks the same. Same haircut. Same shoes. Same clothes. So, after a while, this is your world. You fit in. But you forget that the world outside doesn't look the same as your world."

"So that's how you spotted him. He did not fit with anything you saw in Shepherds Pass. And it means he just got here. Amber must have had to order two last-hit teams before killing the account who could blow the whistle on all of it. That means you have at least one more hitman out there."

"Yeah. If Amber doesn't give him up, he will just leave."

"So, no more payday, and the hitter or hitters go home."

"It also proves the motive to conceal a crime.

So, I figure her lawyer is working on some chickenshit defense for mental strain or incompetence. But if she planned this mess, it shows otherwise."

Wendell ran over to Lavon and Patterson. "Nash and Coleman want me over to the lake to help organize some of the uniforms for crowd control. They found a waitress from the Chinese restaurant floating in the lake with a stab wound."

"Then have a good night because I think I need to lay down before I fall. And tell Nya to thank you for her help."

"I didn't know she helped you."

"I think she did when she visited me at the hospital." Lavon wandered off.

"She never visited you at the hospital."

Wendell stated but Lavon had already walked too far to hear him.

Just as it has been the duty of lighthouses for hundreds of years to guide ships safely into harbors. Thank you for allowing us at the Looking Glass Lighthouse to steer your thoughts dreams and imagination safely to a port of enjoyment.

We are pleased that you have chosen to join us on this journey.

Please feel free to send feedback, questions, and comments to Lookingglasslighthouse@gmail.com and be sure to make your preferred literature vendor aware of your experience.

AS A SPECIAL THANK your for allowing us to entertain you we would like to give you a special sneak peek into the next episode of Shepherds Pass- Revenge at Shepherds Pass

Chapter 1

The US Marshals Service is the oldest law enforcement agency in the United States, having been put into place by George Washington and the First US Congress. It has duties have been modified over the years, but the foundation has remained primarily intact.

On and unseasonably warm fall evening a bus operated by the US Marshals service left the Jefferson City Missouri Federal Courts building bound for Chillicothe women's prison in upstate Missouri. The bus had ten female passengers and three marshals supervising the prisoner return. The old blue due to be retired soon. Marshals bus drove highway 70 first without incidence. As is common in Missouri in the fall even fell quickly and the dark begun to threaten the light. The driver noticed smoke rising from the highway in front of him and lights flashing signaling the highway patrol and possible the fire department.

"Looks like a car fire ahead. Signal the house we are going to be late." The drive commanded one of the guards. It is standard protocol that any deviation from their assigned plan had to be noted and called in to command. After buzzing static and a bad connection the second Mashal confirmed they were free to follow the detour that was being advertised by the highway crew. There was a gowning from the passengers. Usually, any deviation from the daily routine of prisoners is seen as a cause to celebrate however they were sure the delay meant they might miss supper have to wait for day to eat. "Pipe down ladies we are going to miss the same meal you are." The third marshal reassured the prisoners.

The traffic thinned out and there was space between the vehicles, and they wound slowly down an outer road clearly not meant for high-speed traffic. Suddenly there was a flash and a huge boom. The front of windshield of the bus was bullet resistant glass and it shatter. "Oh Shit." The driver yelled. In an instant he knew what was happening. They were under attack. There is no such thing as bullet proof glass, only bullet resistant glass. The first shot to the window must have come from an extremely heavy caliber weapon he thought for it shattered the window. "We're under attack." The drive yelled. The other two marshals stared reaching for their side arms in between prayers. One more 50. Caliber round and the drives window would be compromised, and it would shatter into a polycarbonate dust. It happened almost in a second. The second 50. Caliber round dropped the front windshield and caused the drivers head to explode as the round continued it destructive path. There was screaming from the prisoners as the bus swerved. Any side traffic speeded up and gave the bus a clear path to its demises. The Second Marshal reached over the soup that was now the driver to steer the bus. He knew there was no way to get control of the pedals, so his best bet was to aim the bus for a ditch and hope for the best. The bus hit the ditch and slide on his side. The second marshal climbed out of the door to the bus. His body armor light up and burst as the 50. Caliber round shot through it as if he were wearing a cheap tee shirt. Two large men walked slowly toward the bus. They both had hunting rifles. The third marshal had been knocked unconscious by the crash. The two men pulled the third marshal from the bus and dropped him on the side of the road. "Where is the key to the back and the cuffs?" The first of the large men commanded. The marshal looked at the men as if he was considering his options, as if he had any. The large man smacked the marshal in the face with the butt of the riffle and before the second strike the marshal presented the key. "Thank you." The large man said just before shooting the marshal in the head.

"All right ladies everyone lines up." The second of the large men instructed as they released the women prisoners from the back of the bus. Women prisoner number ten was Julia Poole. Julia Poole rushed to the two men and hugged them. The first of the large men walked over to Willow Rushmore one of the prisoners and handed her some money. "You run in that direction." He commanded.

"What?" Willow seemed totally confused.

"Excuse me sir one of the other women in line." Interrupted. The man looked at the woman interrupting as if his patience was being tested.

"Give me my money and I'm out of here. She aint too bright and time is wasting."

"You understand what we are doing don't you."

"Yelp."

"Why don't you explain it to the class."

"You are going to give us all money and send us in different direction to confuse the hunting dogs they are will be sending."

"You get an A." He handed her money and pointed where she was to run, and she was off without another word. The other women except Julia Poole all excepted their money and was off. Julia stripped off her clothes and handed them to one of the other women the then rubbed herself in a mix that had been brought by the two large men. She then slipped on a jumpsuit from a plastic bag. The mixture she rubbed herself in was made of wild onion. Something found all over the woods, a trick used by runaway slaves during the times of the underground railroad. The trio set fire to the marshal's bus then took off.

Don't miss out!

Visit the website below and you can sign up to receive emails whenever Alex Mitchell publishes a new book. There's no charge and no obligation.

https://books2read.com/r/B-A-UGUAB-EDWOC

BOOKS 2 READ

Connecting independent readers to independent writers.

www.ingramcontent.com/pod-product-compliance
Lightning Source LLC
Chambersburg PA
CBHW031844170626
46807CB00004B/1620

Since the 1960s, Daniela Gioseffi has been an irrepressible and unforgettable voice in many of the key debates in American culture. Her advocacy has given a special validity to her work in the fields of civil rights, women's rights, and of antiwar activism. Her work displays the depth and range of her commitment and contribution to human rights.

— **ROBERT VISCUSI**, Co-Founder and Board Member of the Italian American Writers Association; Professor of English and Executive Officer of the Wolfe Institute for the Humanities at Brooklyn College, CUNY; author of *Astoria* (American Book Award, 1996) and *Ellis Island*, among others

Respected anthologist Daniela Gioseffi [*Women on War: International Voices for the Nuclear Age* (Touchstone Books - Simon & Schuster, 1988; American Book Award) and *On Prejudice: A Global Perspective* (Anchor Books - Knopf Doubleday, 1993, Ploughshares World Peace Award)] — does not just encourage readership toward her humane ideals but backs them up with her own writing.

—AMERICAN BOOK REVIEW

Women on War is an eloquent response which sweeps with authority through time and across national boundaries with authority.

— THE NEW YORK TIMES

Gioseffi, a prizewinning poet, activist, and educator, sets the scene for this invaluable anthology, *Women on War: International Writings from Antiquity to the Present*, in a bracing introduction that traces the enormous shadow militarism casts across our planet and our lives, from the immediate tragedies of war to the environmental damage caused by military industries and the poverty exacerbated by huge military expenditures.

— BOOKLIST